KEROSENE

Also by Chris Wooding:

Crashing
Point Horror Unleashed: *Catchman*
Broken Sky

KEROSENE

Chris Wooding

SCHOLASTIC
PRESS

F

Scholastic Children's Books,
Commonwealth House, 1-19 New Oxford Street,
London WC1A 1NU, UK

a division of Scholastic Ltd
London ~ New York ~ Toronto ~ Sydney ~ Auckland
Mexico City ~ New Delhi ~ Hong Kong

Published in the UK by Scholastic Ltd, 1999

Copyright © Chris Wooding, 1999

Lyrics taken from *Short Straw Fate* are reproduced
by kind permission of Broccoli.

ISBN 0 590 11358 5

Typeset by M Rules
Printed by Cox and Wyman Ltd, Reading, Berks.

10 9 8 7 6 5 4 3 2 1

"I'm weak and I'm filled with contradiction
I'm lost and I'm found
My actions all follow your predictions
I hope that you're satisfied now
More than once I've failed the tests that you prescribe
I don't wanna be around when you decide
Mine's the short straw fate"

Broccoli, *Short Straw Fate*

Contents

Chapter One

Tinder

The bedroom was empty, the sunlight of the late autumn afternoon a pale wash across the crazy-paving pattern of the duvet. A bookshelf stood next to the bed, cluttered with comics, graphic novels, markers, sable brushes, jars full of dirty water and other assorted odds and ends.

The walls and ceiling were black, but they were painted with a variety of bright cartoons, all following the same motif: clocks. Grandfather clocks, alarm clocks (digital and analogue), watches, cuckoo clocks, and more. Some had faces, some were melting in the style of Dali, and some were blank, with no hands or numerals. Some smiled, some leered, some had teeth, some winked. They floated in a starfield, and a few of them had been captured as they drifted behind another, giving the paintings a curious three-dimensional perspective.

On the wall above the bed hung a clay effigy of a tribal wolf-mask, its flat snout snarling emptily. A wardrobe and a chest of drawers leaned against the other wall, groaning under the weight of the junk that had accumulated on top of them. In the centre of the room was a mobile of little wooden baby angels painted brightly with cutesy faces beaming, or with their expressions scrunched up with the effort of blowing their tiny horns. A poster of Larisa Oleynik as Alex Mack was positioned in pride of place opposite the window. A stereo system rested on the floor beside an untidy stack of CDs.

The room was silent.

Then, dimly, there was the sound of a key rattling in a lock downstairs. The latch thudded back, and the front door opened, whining on its hinges. There was a slam as it was closed behind the newcomer, then the sound of footsteps hurrying up the stairs. The door to the bedroom was flung open, and a boy of about sixteen entered, ignoring the "BIOHAZARD" warning sign on the outside. He threw the door closed behind him and slumped down heavily on the edge of the red and white bedspread, his head in his hands, breathing hard.

It was a small, thin figure that sat there for a long while, unmoving. His baggy jeans were scuffed and flecked with bright paint. He wore a heavy-knit black jumper that dwarfed his bony shoulders, and a blue T-shirt beneath. His brown hair stuck out everywhere, an uncontrollable ragtag mop.

"SHIT!" he screamed suddenly, his voice sounding raw and high. He sprang off his bed and kicked his chest of drawers hard, sending rolled-up drawings and

badges toppling off the edge. Unsatisfied, he laid into it viciously, planting the sole of his battered Converse on it again and again. Next he turned his wrath on the blank face of his wardrobe. He swung a punch into it, his fist driven by a desperate need to hit something, *anything*; to vent the frustration that seared through his veins.

The pain brought him back to his senses. He near broke his knuckles with that first punch, so just to spite himself he threw another one with the same hand. At the last moment, he couldn't help pulling the force out of it. His body was instinctively trying to stop him harming himself. But it still connected, hard, and the blaze of agony that exploded in his hand almost made him pass out.

His good hand clamped around his wrist, he sat back down on the bed, his teeth clenched while he fought back the urge to cry, ashamed of the tears that pricked at his eyes. The pain in his hand eventually began to subside; the turmoil in his head did not.

It had been one of *those* days. God, it was so *humiliating*. One of those days when he couldn't look anyone in the eye, when he had walked along the road to his house with his attention fixed firmly on the ground in front of his feet, shuffling meekly along so as not to draw attention to himself.

He had been doing alright all day. And then just on the last stretch, the walk home from the shops, it had all come crashing down on him. He had seen a tall guy with a skinhead wearing tight black jeans and cherry-red Doc Martens, walking along the other side of the road. Mildly interested, he was looking over at him when the guy turned round and met his eye. He had experienced a sudden, unpleasant thrill at being caught staring, and turned his eyes away.

But a moment later, the skinhead had whistled him, a short, sharp *wheep* through pursed lips. He looked back, feeling a terrified nausea creep into his belly, and the skinhead had flicked him the finger, saying: "You wanna photo, mate? Last longer."

He felt it sweep over him like a cloak. Hot blood flushed into his cheeks, prickling heat across his face and the nape of his neck. His throat tightened at the sides, his heart began to pound, he was sweating, he felt sick. He turned away from the skinhead, looking down, wishing he could disappear. The skinhead didn't hassle him any more. But the damage was done.

The remainder of the journey was a nightmare. Everyone on the street seemed to be looking at him. It was as if his affliction marked him out, making everyone stare at him. Like some kind of freak. He was conscious of walking fast, but he couldn't help it. He had to get off the street, away from the piercing glares of the passersby.

When he had finally gained the safety of his house, self-disgust had flooded through him. *Why?* Why so afraid?

Afraid? No. *Shy.*

He snorted, smiling bitterly. A sweet word. When people thought of shy, it was always kind of cute. Nice. Coy girls in floral dresses, wide-eyed cartoon squirrels.

Not a crippling, awful sensation that made your tongue too thick to speak and locked up your brain. But that was what it meant to him. And it unmanned him, made him pathetic and weak and *ashamed*.

Trembling, he got up and walked unsteadily to the drawers that he had battered seconds earlier. The clocks swam around him in the starfield on the walls. With his good hand, he brought out a box of Swan Vesta matches. Crossing the room, he closed the thick blue curtains, shutting out the dull light, plunging himself into darkness.

He sat back down on the bed and pulled out a match. Slowly, speeding up as he got to the end, he drew it along the sandpaper. It sparked first try, flaring white as the phosphorus head caught, then settling to a steady yellow flame. He watched it, fascinated. Shadows flickered deep on his face in the light of the match. The heat of it was comfort to him. He stared into the heart of the flame, and felt some of the frustration drain out of him. There was peace there, at least.

He let the match burn down, only blowing it out when the pain in his fingertips became too much to bear. He sat there in the darkness for a while, feeling better. Flame was such a calming thing. Just a little match, and he felt okay again.

It was enough. For now.

Cal was sitting at the table, his hands wrapped around his third cup of coffee that morning, when the doorbell rang. Joel. He went to get it.

"How you doing?" Joel said as Cal opened the door. "What'd you do to your hand?"

Cal held up his bandaged knuckles with a kind of funny smile. "Someone slammed a door on it."

Joel winced. "Ouch. Lucky he got your knuckles and not your fingers, yeah?"

"Didn't feel lucky at the time."

The taller kid laughed. "Guess not."

"D'you want some coffee? There's still some left in the percolator."

Joel shouldered the Stussy schoolbag he was carrying. The weight was beginning to make his muscles hurt. "We should get going," he said. "Besides, you drink too much of that crap. All that caffeine'll make your bones crumble."

"The price to pay for having the reflexes of a hummingbird," Cal returned.

"And you still can't get to school on time," Joel replied.

"That's 'cause I have to spend so much of my morning drinking coffee."

"Good logic. I think."

"Don't you worry yourself about it. Let me get my bag and we'll go."

Joel and Cal had known each other practically since they were embryos. Their parents had met at antenatal classes, and pretty soon the two couples had become friends of a sort. Cal suspected it was more because his parents were scouting for someone to offload their new kid on during the week while they were in London. They both worked in the City, and though Joel's slightly weird parents were hardly the ideal choice to help raise their child, it was cheaper than an *au pair.*

On his fifteenth birthday, Cal's parents had deemed him mature enough to be allowed to stay in the house on his own during the week. This suited him fine; having a house of his own five days out of seven was not bad for a kid his age. Joel crashed round often, but recently his parents had insisted that he stay at home on weekdays because of his upcoming GCSE mocks.

If it were not for the fact that they had grown up together – largely under the same roof – it would be difficult to imagine them ever being friends. Joel dressed in all the latest street-gear, whereas Cal was permanently scruffy and always looked like he'd just got out of bed. Joel was into jungle and trance music while Cal loved Mega City Four above all other bands. Joel walked with a confident, self-assured swagger while Cal tended to shuffle around with his head down, obsessed with his own thoughts. The differences went on, but somehow they always had the common ground of each other, and never once had either of them tired of that.

"You got a fag you can crash me?" Joel asked.

"You owe me three already, you tight git," Cal replied pleasantly. "And none of your cheesy JPS glass-shards-in-the-filter efforts either. I mean *real* fags."

"*Three fags?* You've got a heart like an abacus, you know that? And you call me tight."

"Yeah, yeah, hand 'em over," said Cal, holding out his good hand, palm up. When Joel hesitated, he said:

7

"I know you got some, I can see them in your shirt pocket."

Joel tutted and pulled the pack of Embassy out. The transparent wrapping hadn't even been taken off them. He grudgingly pulled the rip-tab and opened the pack, then drew out three cigarettes and put them in Cal's waiting hand.

"Never buy twenties, my friend, they'll give you away every time," Cal advised sagely. "Go for the slimmer ten-pack if you want to hide them from me."

"I'll remember that, thanks," Joel replied, drawing out the Focus Point insert for later use, before getting a cigarette for himself and pocketing the pack again.

Cal added two of Joel's cigarettes to his own pack, and sparked up the remaining one with his Clipper (black plastic, with a smiley sun face painted on it in acrylics and varnished over). He lit Joel's fag with it as well, then stared at the flame for a second before reluctantly shutting it off.

"So who is it you've got today?" Joel said. He talked with a slight, gentle lisp. It was due to too much breast-feeding while he was a baby, Joel had explained once with a wicked grin. Apparently, that could make a baby's tongue get used to a particular motion or something, and give it minor difficulties in pronouncing *s* and *z* later in life. Joel was a trove of useless facts like these. But Cal still felt sick at the thought of Joel's mother breastfeeding.

"Mostly it's okay," Cal replied. "Except I've got chemistry with Jock McBastard after dinner. That should be fun."

"Oh yeah. I'm kind of staying out of his way for a bit. He's on a vendetta with me 'cause of my hair."

Joel had recently had his black hair plaited into cornrows. Cal said it made him look like a member of an LA gang, which was just the effect it had been intended to achieve. But Mr McLeder, the chemistry teacher and deputy head (and trainee fascist, Cal was fond of saying) was less than enthusiastic. He had threatened to send Joel to the Head if he didn't take them out.

This didn't much worry Joel; the pitiful long-term memory of the teachers at Bishop Grove was legendary. He reckoned if he kept his head down for a week or so, McLeder would have forgotten all about his warning.

They walked to school under grey and cloudy skies, heavy with the promise of rain. True to their usual routine, they flicked the stubs of their fags over the high garden fence that belonged to the school caretaker before turning down the main drive. Cal didn't know what the poor guy did with all the dog-ends that they'd put into that garden in the last couple of years, but he must be doing *something* with them, or the lawn would be carpeted in filters by now. Popular folklore had it that he collected them for rollups, but Cal didn't believe that even *he* was as scutty as that.

Ahead of them, the featureless brick walls of the school stood blankly beneath a grey slate roof and black plastic guttering. They walked towards the jumble of low buildings and mobiles, and Cal felt a familiar tenseness tighten his chest ever so slightly. He knew somehow that today was not going to be a good day.

Lunchtime, and Cal made his excuses to Joel and disappeared, as he often did. He hated tagging along like a silent shadow while Joel hung around with his other friends. It wasn't that they made fun of him – though they probably did when he wasn't around and Joel was out of earshot – but he just felt so awkward being around them. They were the in-crowd, the guys who smoked down the track at the bottom of the school fields. They wore earrings (left ear only, of course) and puffer jackets, and they went to techno and dance clubs which were fifteen-odd quid a throw to get in.

But when Cal was with them, he couldn't force out his words, and when he did they always sounded painfully stupid to his ears. And then Joel would look kind of embarrassed, even though he was trying not to show it, and Cal would feel twice as bad. After a while, he'd given up trying.

He didn't begrudge Joel his friends, and he knew Joel would never say that he didn't want Cal around; so he began to do the diplomatic thing, and pretend he had some artwork to finish off in the design department or something. Then he would slope off to his favourite set of steps, just outside the fire door to the science block, and sit there, and eat his lunch, and read a book or draw. Nobody ever came to disturb him; the gangs of lunchbreak smokers avoided that particular corner because it was too visible from the teacher's staffroom.

He was quietly munching on his sandwich, leafing through an Orson Scott Card novel that he'd borrowed from the local library, when he became aware of voices approaching him from the direction of the staff car park.

"What about him?" said a male voice. He felt himself begin to flush, aware that he was being looked at, and concentrated furiously on the words on the page.

"That's that kid from 11B," replied a female, her voice dropping not quite enough to avoid being heard.

Now he recognized them. Emma Cobley and her boyfriend, Rob Oakley. He flushed even deeper. Emma Cobley. *Everybody* fancied Emma Cobley. Well, as much as everybody could be said to do anything. There was no question that she was the most desired female in year eleven, at any rate. She was a girl whose physical appearance overcame any objections a kid might have about her character.

"I know who it is, I seen him around," Rob replied impatiently. "I seen him fagging it with his mate before now."

Yeah, thought Cal. Mate. Singular.

The voices got closer, accompanied by the crunch of shoes on gravel-scattered tarmac. Cal didn't look up, but his fingers were digging into his sandwich, making little bready dents.

"Alright, mate?" Rob said, and the question was addressed to him.

"Alright," he mumbled back, not looking up at them, not daring to.

Rob paused for a moment, maybe expecting a better acknowledgement. "Listen, you got a light? Mine's run out."

Cal dipped his hand in his pocket and pulled out his Clipper, holding it out. Rob took it. Still Cal couldn't meet their eyes.

"Cheers," he said uncertainly. "I'll bring it back in a few minutes, okay?"

"Okay," Cal mouthed, but the breath didn't come out to form the words.

"Urgh, what are you *eating*?" Emma exclaimed suddenly, spying the filling in his sandwich.

"Marshma—" he began to reply, the words coming out like a short gasp. He took a breath and started again. "Marshmallow and Coco Pops."

Emma laughed, a high, musical sound. "That is *truly* disgusting. Don't your parents *feed* you?"

Cal didn't reply. He wished they'd go away. They had his lighter, what more did they want?

"Uh . . . yeah," said Rob. "I'll bring this back in a bit." And with that, they turned and walked away, Emma making some comment under her breath to her boyfriend.

He looked up and watched them, once they had their backs to him. Emma Cobley; whether you loved or hated her, there wasn't a boy in the school who hadn't fantasized about what it would be like with her. Baby-doll blonde ringlets, a knee-weakeningly sweet smile, and a ruthlessly aerobicized figure made her the stuff of adolescent dreams. And she knew it. The other girls either orbited her like satellites or spat their envy; the boys just fell at her feet.

She and Rob walked towards the car park, then turned right and went down the narrow alley between a large skip and the swimming-pool building. The skip was full of branches and leaf-cuttings; the school had recently hired in gardeners to trim back some of the trees overlooking the old mud track that ran near by. Emma and Rob had obviously decided that the skip was as good a place as any to hide for a smoke.

Cal looked back at his book, not really seeing the text. The heat was draining slowly out of his face. *Great*, he thought to himself. *Now you've got to wait here till they give you your lighter back.* And just when the only thing he wanted to do was get away. Leaving now would only make him seem more dumb.

He ate the rest of his sandwich. Marshmallow and Coco Pops. So what? Tasted good, anyway.

After a few minutes, they still hadn't returned. It didn't take that long to smoke a fag. Still, rather than have to go and face them again, he immersed himself back in the book, listening with half an ear for the sound of their footsteps.

More minutes passed. Still he waited. Occasionally he threw a glance over at the skip, hoping to see them coming out. The fourth-sitting dinner bell rang, cutting through the bubble of conversation and laughter that filtered over from the playground.

Eventually, he decided that he'd have to go and ask for it back. It wasn't *that* big a deal, going up to them and asking them. They'd just forgotten, that was all. And he'd only painted up that lighter yesterday. He couldn't very well let them walk off with it.

Maybe they won't be there, he thought. *Maybe they've gone while I wasn't looking.*

He got halfway to the skip, then turned around and sat back down again. His heart was thudding. He didn't really want the lighter that badly anyway; let them have it.

No. Go and get it.

Taking a deep breath, he stood up and walked over to the skip. He hesitated for a moment before he got to the narrow alley between the skip and the swimming-pool building. He didn't really have to look in there; he could just wait for a while for them to come out.

Disgusted at himself, he bit the inside of his lip hard. The pain drove away the rebellious thoughts, and he looked into the alley.

Emma and Rob were there alright. They were entwined in each other's arms, Emma's hand sliding up the back of Rob's shirt, kissing each other hungrily. Cal just sort of hung there, staring at them, not daring to break them up but not wanting to go, either. Because he knew he'd never pick up the courage to come back a second time.

Then Emma opened her eyes a little, and they widened as she saw him there. She patted Rob on the shoulder with the palm of her hand, alerting him to Cal's presence. Cal was instantly overwhelmed with embarrassment, his eyes dropping to the floor, and he would have just thrown it all in and run off then if Rob hadn't said: "Oh, your lighter. Sorry, mate, I forgot about it."

"S'okay," he mumbled. Emma slid away from her boyfriend with a smug, serpentine smile, and Rob dug in his pocket and got the lighter out.

"You mind if we light another couple off it? See us through for a bit."

"Sure," he said quietly, shuffling on the spot in agitation.

"Chatty little devil, aren't you?" Emma commented with something that might have been a sneer in her voice. There was a *snick* as Rob lit up a cigarette.

Cal didn't know how to answer that. His fists clenched and unclenched on the inside hems of his long jumper sleeves, sending a steady throb up his arm from his battered knuckles.

"I'll take that as a no," she added, then lit her own cigarette and handed him the Clipper back.

"Cheers, mate," Rob said. "Sorry about forgetting it and that. You want one?"

Cal forced himself to look up, and saw that Rob was offering him a fag from his pack. For a second, visions flashed through his head: he'd have a smoke with them, they'd find out he's really not such a bad kid, maybe they'd hang out a little, then he'd go with Joel and meet *his* friends, and he'd just be normal and not a *failure* any more. . .

But visions were all they were, and all he wanted to do now was escape, get back to his safe, solitary existence.

"No, thanks," he managed to say, and thought how

terse and rude his voice sounded. He turned around clumsily, hastening away from them, but then suddenly a new voice made him halt.

"Mr Sampson! And what were you doing round there?"

It was McLeder.

Chapter Two

Friction

As they stepped out of the Deputy Head's office, Cal remembered the premonition he had experienced that morning. It really wasn't turning out to be a good day for him.

The Deputy Head, Mr McLeder, was a bear of a man. He had dark ginger hair and a moustache, which nestled sternly over his top lip, and he stood at maybe six-three, with wide, rugby-player shoulders. His sheer physical presence was enough to terrify the younger children in the school; his bellowing voice could often be heard right across the playground as he destroyed some unfortunate miscreant.

For Cal, it had been an ordeal he never wanted to repeat. Squirming under the iron gaze of McLeder, he had endured a thorough roasting. Emma and Rob looked suitably abashed, though he could tell they were less than intimidated. But Cal had been in anguish. His heart thumped, his face burned, tears tried to spring to his eyes, he couldn't swallow properly, and he could only respond to McLeder's questions in a tiny voice (which the teacher pretended not to be able to hear, so that he was forced to speak louder). And all the time, he was conscious of Emma's disgusted glances, sneering at how weak he was.

To make it worse, he had chemistry with McLeder next thing. Joy.

Of course, even though he hadn't been smoking, he got into trouble for it. When he protested his innocence, McLeder made him turn out his pockets; and out came his half-full pack of Embassy. He wanted to say that he hadn't *actually* been smoking on school grounds, he hadn't really done anything *wrong*; but his nerve failed him.

"That was brilliant, doofus," Emma said sullenly as they trooped out of McLeder's office towards their form rooms for afternoon registration. "I really *needed* that."

Cal's throat tightened, and he hurried away from them as quickly as he could. His ungracious retreat made him feel like a complete loser; but he couldn't bear another second around them, not after McLeder had demolished him for the day.

"Leave 'im alone," Rob said, watching him go. "It weren't his fault, really."

"I lost my bloody prefect badge because of him!" Emma snapped. "So now, instead of standing by the radiator in the corridor all lunchtime, I'll have to freeze to death outside!" She bunched her slender hands into fists. "That kid makes me sick. I just want to slap him or something. God, he's so *wet!*"

"You're just worked up 'cause we got caught," Rob commented.

"Yeah, and who *got* us caught? That was the perfect hiding-place. If he hadn't been standing there talking to us in full view from the staffroom, we wouldn't have been caught at all."

"Don't know why you're getting so wound up about it."

"You wouldn't," Emma replied acidly.

Rob gave her a look. "I gotta get to form, anyway," he said. "I'll see you after school, right?"

"Maybe."

He shrugged and walked off, indicating that he didn't care either way. Emma gritted her teeth and made a little noise of frustration. They had been going out for four months now, and she still hadn't cracked him. How could he be so *blasé* about their relationship? She could have virtually any other boy in the school, and they would fall over themselves to please her. What did it say about her character, that she had chosen the only one who couldn't be bothered to attend to her moods, and didn't seem to care when she threatened to break up with him?

It says I'm a retard for going out with him in the first place, she thought to herself.

But it was deeper than that. It was a challenge. Rob intrigued her, because he wouldn't adore her; he always acted like he was only with her because there was nothing better to do. He stood her up occasionally, bad-mouthed her sometimes to his mates, and refused to meet her parents; but while this pissed her off something special at the time, it was also part of the reason she was attracted to him. The other boys were, well, too *easy*.

In fact, she thought nastily as she pushed open the door to her form room, *I bet that mumbling little dickhead from 11B would just burst his balls if I started coming on to him.*

She sat down in her seat, next to Abby Cohen. Abby was a new girl, in from St Paul's on the other side of town. Emma didn't usually mix with new girls until they had established themselves in the pecking order; but Mrs Denton, Emma's form teacher, had a thing for making people sit in alphabetical order. To separate troublemakers, she said, and to help them all to get to know people they wouldn't normally talk to.

So Abby Cohen and Emma Cobley had been forced to sit together, and they'd hit it off pretty much straight away. Abby was surprisingly with it, considering she was from St Paul's and everything; she dressed cool, she listened to all the right music, and she knew some pretty important faces around the nightclub scene. Emma reckoned that she had the potential to be something of a heavily-desired catch once she got herself settled, and figured it was better to have the girl on her side than off it.

Abby was a good-looking girl, no mistake about that. She had one of those kind of *sculpted* faces, and wide copper-coloured eyes. Her straight hair was so black that it sheened under the striplights, and she wore baggy dungarees over a loose T-shirt, and fat trainers.

She said hi to Emma as she sat down, and Emma

recounted the incident with Cal and McLeder, breaking off once to call out "Here," as Mrs Denton droned out her name from the register. Abby tutted in all the right places and lent her a sympathetic ear, and then the form dispersed and they made their way to their classes.

"I think I've got that kid you were talking about in my next lesson," Abby said as she and Emma walked through the corridors, surrounded by the echo of the nattering year seven brats as they poured out of an adjacent classroom. "He's in my chemistry set. He does art, too."

"McLeder called him Calhoun or something."

"Yeah, Cal Sampson. That's his name. I've seen him with that other kid, you know, the one who wants to be black. . ."

"Joel Manning?" Emma said, then laughed out loud. "Wants to be *black*?"

Abby smiled in response. "You know, he dresses like a homey, and he listens to all that jungle stuff, and now he's done his hair in cornrows like Snoop Doggy Dogg used to have." She lifted up clumps of her own hair to emphasize. "And he hangs around with all the *rude boys*." She said this last phrase in an exaggerated Jamaican accent, and kept it running through her next sentence: "And he be smoking de *'erb,* mon, so I be told." Reverting to her normal voice, she finished with a shrug: "I just think he wants to be black, that's all."

Emma was shaking her head. "I dunno where you come up with this."

"Hey, do you wanna detour and check out the art

display? They're putting up the big competition results today," Abby said, suddenly changing the subject.

"Yeah, okay, I've only got RE next anyhow."

They made their way through the press of bodies hustling their way to their next lesson. The air was full of the sound of chatter and the squeak of shoes on the bare stone floor. A girl from year eight clipped Emma's bag as she rushed past, jolting her arm. Emma tutted loudly, grimacing her displeasure.

"Little shits get more rowdy every year," she commented.

Abby made a resigned noise of agreement.

The traffic in the corridors thinned out as they ambled across the school. Abby was conscious that she was going to be late for chemistry, but McLeder never turned up for ten minutes after the period started anyway. She wanted to see the art competition results. Back at St Paul's, she had been the pride of the art department, and her smooth, swirling style was lauded by her teachers. She was virtually guaranteed an A when her GCSEs came around in June. And though she didn't like to be big-headed, she was quietly confident that she could slaughter the competition here, too.

"Y'know, this reminds me. About that kid, Cal. I saw him a couple of days ago at lunchtime in the art rooms. He was just starting his picture for the competition. Most of us have been working on them for weeks. I dunno why the teachers go so easy on him; he's always late with his work."

"Probably feel sorry for him," Emma said.

"Why, what's wrong with him?" Abby asked, interested.

"Dunno if there's anything *wrong* with him. He's just spineless. Probably got an overprotective mother."

"Really? I mean, he always seems pretty quiet. Doesn't say anything to anyone except his mate. You reckon he's got something up with his head?"

"No," Emma replied, looking faintly tired at having to repeat herself. "He's just a wimp, is all."

The display was up on the main corridor, opposite the art department and just inside the school doors. They skipped by the sections for the younger years, only occasionally stopping to laugh at how out of proportion someone's charcoal self-portrait was, or how feeble their still-life fruit bowls were. The year eleven work was at the end; each one had a percentage mark and a name attached to it, and the top three had a little rosette reading 1st, 2nd or 3rd.

Abby scanned her eyes eagerly over the paintings and pictures; and then her face dropped.

"I don't believe it," she said, annoyed. "That cocky sod."

Her picture was of an old house on a hill, a thin stream winding its way down through grassy meadows. In the far right foreground there was one half of the face of a milkmaid, her eyes bent downwards as if attending to something. It was an unusual angle and perspective, and painted with great care and skill. Certainly, it was head and shoulders above most of the pictures on display. The tag declared it to be by Abby

Cohen, and gave it a mark of 96%. But the little blue rosette on it put it into second place.

Next to it was a violent charcoal drawing, a close-up of a terrified mouse as a falcon swooped down to snatch it up, its talons only inches away. It was grotesquely exaggerated: the falcon looked more like a dragon, with enormous, vicious claws and a hateful expression on its face, while the mouse gave the impression of utter helplessness, its black eyes frozen in their final moment. The style was incredibly urgent and messy, as if it had been scrawled in a frenzy, but somehow clear detail seemed to show through the tangle of lines and smudges. The whole picture gave off an impression of great speed and power.

Beneath its red first-place rosette, was written: Cal Sampson, 98%.

"Oh, that gets on my *nerves*," Abby said. "That thing only took him a couple of days, if that. I spent *ages* on mine. Look, it's just a *scribble.* That spawny bastard! How could they give him ninety-eight for that? It's not even got any colour in it!"

"He beat yours with *that*? It's crap," Emma said.

"Yeah, cheers, make me feel better," Abby replied sarcastically, not taking her eyes off the picture. It wasn't that he'd beat her, it was just that he'd beat her so *effortlessly*. . .

"Must be like you said. The art department are soft on him."

"It's so completely not fair," Abby moaned.

"Best do something about it, then," said Emma, with

a wry note in her voice that made Abby tear her attention away from the picture.

"Like what?"

Emma paused to greet one of Rob's friends, favouring him with a scorching smile as she did so. That lad fancied her desperately and wasn't very good at hiding it. Maybe she should flirt with him a bit more; a touch of healthy competition might get Rob into gear. When he was gone, she turned back to Abby.

"Way I see it, he's condemned me to a winter of freezing out on the playground, and he's shown you up without any trouble at all."

"He hasn't really shown me *up*. . ." she began, but Emma continued over her half-hearted protest.

"So I was thinking, right, we can't let something like that slide. That little retard's got it coming. Let's give it to him."

"So what do we do?" asked Abby. The idea of a little gentle revenge didn't seem so bad to her right then; she was still smouldering from being beaten so easily, and he *had* got Emma into trouble.

"Well, have you ever seen him with a girl? Or even talking with a girl?"

"Don't think so," Abby replied, unsure as to where this was all leading.

"I reckon it'd be nice if a couple of girls suddenly developed a crush on our friend Cal," Emma said, with a look of cruel cunning in her eyes.

Abby caught on after a few blank-faced seconds. "A couple of girls like us?" she suggested, mock-innocently.

"Uh-huh. Just like us. And by the time we both blow him out, his head'll be so screwed he won't know *where* he is."

Abby grinned. Harmless fun. She liked it. "Okay," she said, and they both pulled an exaggerated pout at each other. "Let's get him."

"He *really* hates me now," Cal said, trudging along next to Joel. The grey, overcast sky hung over them, miserable and depressing. They were walking back home through the estates that surrounded the school, featureless brick flats and endless houses that all looked identical except for the varying amount of debris in the tiny front gardens. "I mean, he hated me before, but now he's got passion."

"All that lesson I thought he was gonna make me take my hat off," Joel commented. "If McLeder'd seen my hair in the mood he was in, he'd have gone skep on me."

"I don't get it. What's he got against me anyway?" Cal said, continuing his own train of thought. "And now he knows I smoke . . . he's gonna turn me into Ryvita if he catches me again."

"Yeah, but you don't smoke at school, do you?" Joel pointed out. "See, you've got what psychologists call a non-addictive personality."

"You're just *brimming* with bullshit today," Cal replied.

"Nah, listen, it's a fact. They reckon that addiction is mainly psychological. Now, you see *me*, I can't go all day at school without grabbing a fag at lunchtime or I start going nuts. But you've been smoking, what, two years?"

"Dunno."

"And you don't get any craving for them at all, do you? I bet you could just stop right now."

"Probably," Cal said, shrugging. "But what would we have to do then? We'd have to take up crack. And I can't afford that on my meagre income."

"Meagre? Your parents give you more than mine do. And it's not like you spend it on clothes, you filthy tramp."

"Yeah, I know, I spend it on fags to keep your grasping hands supplied," Cal returned.

He loved these little verbal duels he fought with his friend. It made him feel normal. Just hanging around and messing about. Trouble was, he had been seeing less and less of Joel lately, as Joel had been getting in with his other crowd, going off to clubs more often and such. He didn't blame him – they certainly seemed more interesting company than he was – but it made him feel a little sad.

They turned off the road on to a little paved plaza, where a few lonely benches were scrawled with predictable graffiti and obscenities, and a row of three shops stood gloomily. A group of three older lads were hanging around one of the benches. One of them looked up uninterestedly as Cal and Joel appeared, and then suddenly his face hardened.

"Oi, you!" he shouted, scrambling to his feet.

Cal and Joel looked at each other and ran. They didn't even have to think about it. There was something in his tone, and in the way he had sprung off the bench, that said he didn't intend a friendly chat when he caught them.

"Go round this way!" Joel said, as their feet pounded the tarmac beneath them. Behind, the other lads had taken up the chase; they came sprinting out of the plaza and on to the road.

"Get back 'ere!" came the cry from behind them, but Cal had no intention of doing that. Who the hell *were* these guys, anyway? He vaguely remembered seeing them around the estate a few times, but he didn't know their names and he had been *sure* they hadn't known his. The suddenness of it all was still catching up with him. One minute they were walking along, doing nothing special, and the next they get jumped on!

When he had thought earlier that it was gonna be a bad day, he hadn't known the half of it.

They raced off the pavement and into an adventure playground, its floor covered with that special shock-absorbent matting that they had to put around places where children might fall off swings and slides. Joel dodged around a brightly-painted witch's hat, with Cal close behind, and sprang over the low metal fence at the far end. Cal followed, the apparatus of the play-ground rushing past him, and vaulted on to the turf on the other side. His ankle buckled awkwardly on the soft ground, and for a moment his foot turned inward; but he lurched on, getting his foot back on track, and carried on running.

The lads behind them were swearing at them, wasting their breath. That was fine with Cal. What wasn't fine was the fact that all three were quite a lot taller than him, and he was only short and couldn't run particularly fast. Joel was pacing ahead, the distance between him and Cal widening even as the gap between Cal and their pursuers closed.

They fled on to another road, running across it at an angle towards a narrow jitty between two gardens. Cal's eyes were fixed on Joel; he almost didn't see the red Cavalier bearing down on him until he heard the squeal of brakes and the blare of a horn. His chest lurched painfully with the shock, and he checked his run automatically as the bonnet screeched past him, just centimetres in front of his thighs, and then shuddered to a halt.

The driver was already getting out, his face knotted in rage, fumbling with his seat-belt release; but Cal was right out of there before he could get the door open, running around the front of the car and into the jitty that Joel had gone through. He was only a few moments too late to avoid being seen by the older lads as they burst out on to the road, and with a cry they took up the pursuit again.

Cal rushed down the jitty, the boards of the high garden fences blurring past on either side. The rapid thudding of the older lads' trainers was too close; at any second, he expected to be tripped from behind and set upon. His arms pumped with the effort of maintaining his speed. He was getting tired now, an ache settling into his thighs, and he felt himself beginning to flag.

What did they *want*, anyway?

And then the jitty opened out into a tiny park area, with a few stout trees spreading their knotted limbs, ragged with brown leaves. Cal caught a fleeting glimpse of Joel as he turned the corner at the far end, and then he was pelting after him along the narrow path. Someone shouted for him to stop again, but he wasn't *that* stupid. At least the voice didn't sound as close as he'd imagined them to be; but he didn't dare spare a second to look over his shoulder as he darted out of the park, down a short dirt slope, and back on to the path.

Now they were running parallel to the old freight railway line. A double set of tracks rested at the bottom of a wide, grassy bank. On the other side was a factory estate, in which he could see a few forklifts and trucks moving slowly around. Past that was the road which led on to where Cal and Joel lived, in the more up-market part of town.

Joel was already scrambling across the tracks; he could really run when he wanted to, Cal gave him that. But Cal didn't have enough of a lead on his pursuers to get away from them, and he was tiring fast.

And then Cal noticed the rumbling that had been gradually getting louder over the last few seconds. He glanced up the tracks, and saw a stolid, square yellow diesel hauling a caterpillar of coal trailers towards them. It wasn't coming fast, but it was fast enough for him.

Before he knew what he was doing, he had turned off the path and was skidding down the slope towards the tracks, following in Joel's footsteps.

The train is coming, a voice in his head told him with quiet urgency.

Behind him, they hadn't given up; they were still after him, sliding down the bank, their trainers finding it hard to get a grip on the moist grass and loose dirt.

The train is coming.

Cal looked up, and the train was a whole lot bigger and nearer than he'd expected it to be (but then, he hadn't really *thought* about what he was doing) and in that moment his scrabbling feet finally lost their precarious purchase on the grass, and he toppled backwards on to his bottom and rolled down the slope, accompanied by a shower of mud.

THE TRAIN IS COMING! the voice in his head screamed, as the world spun around him.

And then his uncontrollable descent was roughly stopped by ground, and though he hit it at a shallow angle, it really hurt. His wrist rested on something cold and hard; bars of wood pressed into his stomach and ribs. He had cracked his damaged hand, and it blasted white-heat agony at him.

THE TRACKS! YOU'RE ON THE TRACKS!

Now those older lads were shouting at him with a different tone in their voice, a tone of fear, and the realization of where he was jerked him into action like an electric shock. A low, booming horn shattered the sky all around, and he scrabbled to get his feet under him, and Joel was screaming at him from the other bank, and he caught the swiftest glimpse of the front of the diesel, huge and terrifying, too, *too* close. . .

And then he was gone, his foot pushing off against

the hard edge of a sleeper and throwing him forward on to his shoulder as the enormous din of the diesel train bellowed over the spot where he had been a second ago.

For a few seconds, that massive wall of noise was all there was, and he heaved in great breaths of relief. Then Joel was next to him, running back over the other set of tracks, squatting down urgently next to him.

"Cal? You alright? Cal?"

"I'm okay, it's alright, I'm okay," he said. His hands were beginning to tremble a little as the adrenalin comedown set in.

"Shit, man, you scared the life out of me," Joel said, and the expression on his face showed that he meant it. "Come on, let's go before the end of that train comes around."

The train was the only thing that separated them from their pursuers now, a clacking, roaring barrier of motion.

"Sure, just gimme a few seconds," Cal muttered.

"Let's *go*!" Joel insisted, hauling him to his feet. Together, they clambered up the bank and away, leaving the older lads far behind them.

"Doing that, though . . . that was a *dumb* thing."

Cal grimaced. "Okay, can we shut up about it now?" he said irritably, looking his bandaged hand over. He pressed it gently with the tips of his fingers and winced. "If I hadn't fallen I'd have made it, no problem. And it worked, didn't it?"

"You nearly got yourself killed!"

"Big deal," Cal said. "Every time you go out to a club with your mates and drop a Dove, *you* take a risk with your life. We're all gonna go sometime. Me, I'd rather it was fast like that than going out on a kidney dialysis machine with my head all screwed up on chemicals."

"It's not the same thing, and don't be an asshole," Joel snapped back. "Doesn't it bother you?"

"Right now?" Cal asked, slouching along with his good hand thrust deep in his pocket. "No, not really."

"Yeah, you're full of it. Wounded martyr."

"Screw you."

"I would, but your momma's coming over tonight."

Cal stopped, throwing his hands up in the air. "Look, is this *going* somewhere? This is a really great chat and all, but I really do have to hoover the lint from under my bed, so if you don't have anything to say, I'm going home."

"Like what?"

"Like who were those guys anyway?"

"How should I know?"

"Well, they were trying to kill one of us, and I know *I've* never met them before."

"It was *you* they were chasing, Cal," Joel pointed out.

"Only 'cause you were so far ahead they couldn't have found you without a radar."

"Jeez, are you mad about *that*?"

"Not really," Cal replied, then looked up into his friend's eyes. "There's no point us both getting pounded, is there?"

"You *are* mad, you always go the martyr when you get mad about something."

"Are you gonna stop calling me that?" Cal snapped.

They walked on for a few moments, as the houses around them became gradually more and more expensive and well-maintained, family homes for the most part, with saloon cars in the drives.

"Why don't you come out to Poppy's tonight?" Joel said at length.

"You know what I'm like around people, Joel," Cal said, exasperated.

"That's all in your head," the other insisted.

"Well, obviously it is. It's hardly gonna be in my *pants*, is it? Still doesn't mean I can do anything about it, though."

"Look, we'll take it slow to start, okay? Just you and me, go to a couple of pubs. You're always okay with a few drinks inside you."

Cal looked doubtful.

"Or we could get a few in at your house, smoke a couple of joints or something. You'll be okay after that."

"My parents come back on Friday evenings," Cal said.

"So we'll go out the back garden," Joel replied expansively. "The house won't smell of smoke. Come on! You've got to get over it *sometime*."

Get over it, Cal thought. *Yeah, I suppose I do.*

And maybe it was because he'd had such a bad day, or perhaps it was because he was still breathless from his brush with the train, but suddenly he really did want to go out tonight. Like Joel said, as long as they took it easy it'd be alright. And he hadn't been out for a long time.

A nervy smile twitched at the edge of his mouth. Joel saw it, and a grin lit up his own face.

"I *knew* you were gonna come. Nice one, Cal! You'll love it, I promise you."

Chapter Three

Spark

There was a queue outside Poppy's when they arrived. Cal wanted to leave, but Joel wouldn't let him.

"You're coming into this bloody nightclub if I have to stuff you in a box and mail you in," Joel said. He was used to having to talk Cal into going places; the most minor discouragement was enough to crumble his frail nerve. Even after they'd had a few drinks, sitting away in a corner at the Screeching Weasel, he'd been jittery. Still, he'd got over the worst of it by now. It was just that the sight of so many people outside meant that Poppy's would be packed, and that awakened all of his fears again.

Joel understood what Cal was like. He sympathized, too. But he knew from experience that sympathy wasn't what Cal needed; he needed someone to push him, someone who wouldn't let him cave in when he got shy. Maybe Joel was unnecessarily harsh sometimes, but it was a case of being cruel to be kind. And also, well . . . he had to admit, sometimes he just got sick of the way Cal acted. His patience only stretched so far.

Cal joined the queue while Joel ran off to get them a couple of cans of lager from the off-licence around the corner. He stared at his shoes while he waited, or gazed off into the middle distance, unwilling to make eye contact with anyone. The pints he'd drunk at the pub had made him more relaxed, but he still felt trapped, penned in by the other people in the queue.

He concentrated on staying where he was, counting the seconds until Joel returned to lend him his strength again. He always felt better when Joel was around; just his being there made him better able to conquer his shyness.

And then Joel did come back, handing him a can as he rejoined him. Cal popped it and swigged greedily.

"How you holding up?" Joel asked.

"Alright," Cal replied after a moment.

"Cool. You ready to drink like a trooper and pull like a demon?"

Cal smiled. "How about if I just drink like a trooper?"

"Halfway there. We'll see to the other half later," Joel replied, his face scrunching up in an exaggerated wink.

"What, we going back to your house to hump yo momma?" Cal beamed. Joel choked on his lager and turned away just in time to avoid spraying it all over the girl in front of them.

"You complete bastard," he said, still laughing as he wiped his mouth. "Don't *ever* talk about my mum while I'm swallowing. And *don't*," he said, raising a finger to forestall his friend. Cal shut his mouth. "I know what you're gonna say, so don't, alright?"

"Sure," Cal replied.

"Urrgh, I feel violated just thinking about it," Joel muttered.

"Everyone needs to be violated once in a while," Cal continued in a conversational tone. "Take your momma, for instance. . ."

The queue crawled forward, until after about half an hour they were finally ushered past the bouncers. The booming throb of the bass pulse pumped through the black walls of the tiny foyer as they paid their entrance fee to the cashier, an attractive Indian girl in a black Kappa top.

Then they walked through the archway and into Poppy's, and the sound swelled all around them, immersing them. A dancefloor swam in dry ice under a swooping pattern of coloured spotlights, clotted with a grooving mass of bodies. The nearby bar – one of three – was an island of light in the surrounding dark-ness of benches, tables, alcoves and steps.

A black metal stairway to their right led to the upper level. They took it, heading for the areas where it was a little quieter and less packed. This was more for Cal's benefit than Joel's, but Joel pretended it was his idea.

The upper level was an enormous balcony that ringed the dancefloor, set with chairs and tables. Miraculously, Joel spotted an empty alcove almost straight away, and he dispatched Cal to claim it while he got them drinks. He took a while to return – he'd met a guy he knew at the bar and spent a few minutes catching up – but Cal felt safe and isolated in his little out-of-the-way spot, and was content to watch people going by from his haven of darkness.

"Quite a few people here tonight," Joel said as he sat down. Cal raised an eyebrow, as his mouth was occupied with the fag he was lighting. "Saw your pal Emma over near the bar."

"Mmm, *just* the person I want to meet," Cal replied, blowing out smoke.

"Come on, it wasn't that bad," Joel said. "Most people would kill to get that amount of attention from her."

"Yeah, only 'cause she hates my guts." He grinned. "It's kind of like my Negative Pull Potential. I have this aura that actively repels attractive females."

"I dunno, maybe it's better that way," Joel replied sagely. "I reckon a girl like Emma would be more trouble than she's worth."

They looked at each other for a moment. "Naah," they said in chorus, and fell about laughing.

They sat around talking for a while, and got a few more drinks in, and Joel even managed to persuade Cal to get up and dance to a song or two. It felt good. And despite all his earlier misgivings, he was having a laugh. When they sat back down, exhausted but happy, he was feeling a whole lot better about himself.

"Listen, I've got a few people I have to say hi to, so I'm gonna dart for a minute," Joel said as he finished the remainder of the drink he'd left. "You wanna come, or are you gonna be alright on your own for a bit?"

"Nah, don't mind me," Cal said, magnaminously. "You go off and have fun, young man."

"Thanks, Pops," Joel said, and then turned away and began worming his way through a knot of people towards another table.

Cal sat back against the padded armrest of the alcove and stretched out along the bench. Sometimes, in moments like this, he felt almost normal again, as if the crushing curse of his shyness was just a bad memory. But he knew that it was a false hope. Tomorrow, he'd be just as he always was, meek and awkward again. The thought put a dent in his bouyant mood.

Maybe he should see a counsellor, he mused. Maybe that would help. Joel had suggested it a couple of times, but Cal had always put it off because . . . well, he didn't know why, really. Perhaps it was because he didn't want to face the thought that he really did have a problem; he wanted to believe that it would go away on its own if he let it.

Or maybe it was because he hated the thought of having to tell his parents about it. He reckoned they'd have to pay something towards it if he tried to get help. But the idea of being a burden to them was more than he could take right now. After all, hadn't they done their best to forget about him since the moment he was born?

Okay, maybe that was a touch melodramatic, but the fact remained that they were *never there.* All week they were in London, and sometimes over the weekends too, when they had special meetings. When they did come back, they barely took an interest in him, instead talking about what they did during the week, what contracts they had closed and who they had lunched with.

Cal rarely stuck around to listen. He went upstairs and painted or read or something.

So, his parents . . . they were pretty much a last resort. And right at the moment he felt okay, so he resolved to worry about it later. Instead, he settled back to watch the mini-world of Poppy's go by around him; couples kissing, people arguing, others drinking and laughing, all to the tempo of the music thumping out of the speakers, a constant background noise.

"Hey," came a voice from near by, and he looked up and saw – to his shock – Emma Cobley standing there. She was wearing a pink cotton crop-top jumper with long sleeves which revealed her bare midriff, and a white silk knee-length skirt. With her baby-doll curls, and the coy smile on her face, Cal thought she looked positively angelic; but that thought was followed by a sudden cautionary question: *What does* she *want?*

"Umm . . . hey," he said, taking a nervous swig of his lager.

"Mind if I sit down?" she purred.

Cal slid his legs down off the bench, making room for her. He watched her cautiously as she sat down next to him. She glanced at him as she was arranging herself and caught his eye; he flicked his gaze away automatically. He was waiting for the familiar flood to swell inside him, the pounding heart, the sweaty palms, the paralysed tongue . . . but mercifully, it did not come. He glanced at the pint of Carlsberg he was holding and sent silent thanks to brewers of alcohol everywhere.

"Okay, look, I'm sorry about today," she said. "I was

just mad. You know, about getting caught and stuff. And I took it out on you a bit, I suppose. Sorry."

"S'okay," he murmured.

"Well, no, it's not really," she replied, knitting and unknitting her fingers. "I do feel sorta bad about it. I was a bitch. I want to . . . you know, make it up to you."

"What do you care?" Cal said, the words escaping him automatically as he thought them. He realized it was pretty rude, but he also knew that he wanted an answer. This whole situation was awfully weird.

"I *do* care," she said, looking wounded. "You know, I might have this *image* of being some kind of heartless cow to you, but I'm really—"

"I don't think that," Cal interrupted quietly.

"Well, good, because I'm not," she said. "Anyway, I just wanted to say I'm sorry and stuff."

"Okay," Cal replied.

"Well, am I forgiven or what?"

"Sure," he said, shrugging.

Emma looked momentarily put out by his apparent lack of interest, but she quickly rallied. "There's something else I wanted to tell you, too," she said. "I know you're probably not interested, but I promised her I'd say something. You know my friend Abby? She's in your chemistry set."

Cal pretended to think for a minute. He knew who she meant. Hadn't he spent enough time watching her from across the lab, admiring the way she brushed her hair behind her ear when she was concentrating? Hadn't he spent enough time screwing himself up with thoughts of her and him? "I think so," he replied after a few seconds.

"She likes you," Emma said.

"No she doesn't," Cal replied.

"Whaddya mean, no she doesn't?" said Emma, taken aback. "I should know, she told me."

"Yeah, I bet she did," said Cal, looking into the depths of his diminishing pint glass.

"You're just kind of . . . unapproachable. Otherwise she'd have said something herself. But seeing as I kind of met you today, she asked me to say for her. I'm telling the truth!"

Cal looked across the bar, hoping desperately for Joel's return. Where *was* he, anyhow? "Whatever," he said. Yeah *right*; as if he was gonna believe for one second what Emma was telling him.

"Fine, I told her you wouldn't be interested," Emma said.

"I'm not interested if you're just trying to take the piss," Cal replied. "Leave me *alone* or something."

Emma shut up for a moment. Cal had surprised her by replying with more than five words. After a time, during which Cal pointedly ignored her presence, she leaned a little closer and said, "So does that mean you *would* be interested if I *wasn't* taking the piss?"

"Well, you are, aren't you?" Cal snapped. "So I guess we'll never know."

"I'm not hearing a straight denial out of you," Emma persisted.

"Shut up," Cal replied.

"Because if you don't like her, I know someone else who likes you as well."

She waited for Cal to ask who, but he wasn't going to give her the satisfaction.

He hated the way she made him feel, so awkward and clumsy and helpless. He wanted to leave, but he didn't know where Joel was; and he didn't much fancy trawling through the minefield of foreign stares that was Poppy's to find him.

"Look, I'm just trying to make it up to you, okay?" Emma said, suddenly cold. "If you don't care, fine. I'll go."

But as she got up to leave, there was something inside him that squeaked in alarm, something that was saying: *She could be telling the truth. She could really be trying to show she's sorry. She might want to be friends. She may be telling the truth about Abby.* And even though every fibre of his being told him that she was not, she was *lying*, she was playing a trick on him, he knew that he'd never be able to live with himself if he blew a chance like this. There wouldn't be another. He had to find out, even if it meant walking into her trap.

Shit, he hated himself for doing this.

"Wait," he said.

"What?" Emma said, pausing.

"Sometimes . . . I get snappy with people I don't know," he said. It was true. When he got shy, the only other defence he had apart from escape was in lashing out at people. He was capable of saying the most cruel and hurtful things when he was cornered. He'd held

44

back with Emma, because he wasn't sure of her true intentions, but a little of it had leaked through, and he'd certainly been pretty short with her.

"Right," Emma said. "You do."

"Look, I mean . . . if you really *mean* it, what you said, you can sit back down if you want." Cal could hardly believe the words were coming out of his mouth. He was drunk, he realized. So, in fact, was she.

Emma eyed him warily for a second, then sat. "Okay." She looked at him. "So, you here with Joel or what?"

"Uh-huh. He's gone off to meet someone. He—"

"Oh, wait," Emma said suddenly. "Abby's coming over." She took up his hands urgently, and looked into his eyes. "Listen, you can't let on that you know. About her. I wasn't supposed to tell you yet."

Cal barely heard her. All he knew was the warm pressure of her smooth hands on his, clasping them hard. "Okay," he said, from somewhere distant.

Then she released him, and he was back to himself again.

Abby sat down with them, carrying three drinks with her. She was wearing baggy jeans and a black T-shirt with a single white stripe that ran vertically over one shoulder.

"Hey, what's up?" she said.

Emma separated the Malibu and Cokes that Abby had brought, and pushed the pint of beer over to Cal. "From me to you," she said, smiling.

"Yeah, Emma sent me to get some drinks while she

went over to you, like I'm her personal slave or something," Abby said cheerily.

Cal looked around. *Joel, where are you?* He needed him there right then, needed his support; but Joel was nowhere to be seen.

"Whoa, hang on, Matt and Kerry are here," Emma exclaimed suddenly. "I've gotta go and talk with them. Hold the fort, willya?" With that, she squeezed around the table and past Abby, snatched up her drink and disappeared.

Cal looked at the floor. Could she have been any more *obvious*? He began to mentally squirm under the awkward silence that followed.

"So, uh, I saw your picture up today," Abby ventured, brushing her hair behind her ear.

"Yeah?" said Cal; then, suddenly animated, he said: "Yeah, I saw yours, too. I loved it. You paint, like, really well with those sort of long, whirly strokes you do with your brush. It's got this really unusual perspective on it, too." He looked away, fading a little. "Better than mine. Mine's just dead straightforward."

Abby smiled. Evidently she'd hit a subject he was passionate about. "Nah, yours is like . . . a total other *style*. It's not worse, it's just different."

She caught herself. Now she was *defending* his picture? It was an automatic reaction to the unexpected compliment, but still, hypocrite was too kind a word for her.

"So, what was Emma saying?" Abby said, feigning ignorance.

"Saying sorry, I think," Cal replied.

"You *think*?"

Cal stopped himself. He could hardly tell Abby about his doubts. "Just saying sorry," he finished, and for some reason his mind strayed to the feeling of Emma's touch on his hands again.

"Yeah, she was feeling pretty guilty about what happened," Abby said. "Like you had enough on your plate and didn't need her getting on your case."

"Yeah, well," Cal said, not really knowing what else to say. He could feel it happening to him again, he was getting tongue-tied. After all, he'd often watched Abby across the room in chemistry, had frequently thought about her when he should have been thinking about covalent bonding of atoms, but she'd always been – like Emma – this . . . almost fantasy being. A creature so far away, so alien to him that to talk to her was like trying to grab a sunbeam. For him, anyway. She existed in a different world from him, and now here she was, being *friendly* even, and it was too much for him. Just once, he'd liked to have been cool and been alright, talked to her and had a good time. But he couldn't.

She cocked her head at him and smiled. "You know, I don't think I've ever actually seen you up close before. You kinda keep yourself hidden at school. You're alright."

"Bad disco lighting," he mumbled, blushing.

She caught his words and laughed. "Yeah, whatever. You know, Emma had sort of said that about you, but I'd not really paid any attention."

"Said what?" Now he was getting short of breath.

"That she thought you were, you know, okay-looking. She'd seen you around a few times and – hey, what's up?"

But Cal was stumbling to his feet, the flood bursting its dam inside him, and he just about managed to gasp "I gotta go," before he was away, pushing through the crowds of people, looking for the exit. Joel or no Joel, he had to get out. Now. Those *bitches*! He knew they were playing with him. He'd almost allowed himself to believe that Abby had fancied him, but to believe that Emma had said that, too? No. It was all crap. They were winding him up. Well, he hoped they got a great fat kick out of it, because they'd succeeded pretty well.

Faces came and went out of the darkness and the flashing, sweeping lights, but he paid no attention to anything except his own panic. The faces terrified him now; every laugh seemed to be directed at him, every scowl, as if the whole nightclub was watching him as he fled, mocking him or hating him. The music degenerated into a noiseless jumble. He vaguely saw suits, the suits of the bouncers that stood at the door, and then he hurried past them, and mercifully they paid him no mind.

Then he was out in the night air, back on the street. He took a few deep, shaky breaths and began to walk. First one step, then another, then –

"Cal? What are you doing out here?"

He almost cried with relief. It was Joel.

The route from Poppy's back to the estate where they lived was a long and circuitous route by road. They'd long since learned that the best way back – short of a taxi – was by cutting across country. With Cal in the state he was in, Joel knew there was no way he could take being in a taxi; so they walked. It was only a mile or so in a straight line, and the night was warm, and besides, he needed to chill out.

After a time, they came across the enormous hay-barn that signified the last field before they came on to the dirt track that rejoined the road near their homes. There they sat down, their backs against the slatted boards. The sky was crystal clear, and the stars shone brighter than either of them had ever seen before. A soft, warm breeze ruffled the long grass around them. The only sound was the stirring of the trees that lined the nearby track, and the distant *swoosh* of cars passing by on a dual carriageway, far to their left.

Joel pulled out some papers and began rolling up a joint. He figured Cal would need one to calm him down. He'd never seen his friend in such a state as when he had first stumbled out of the nightclub. Most of the walk back had been in silence, with Cal wrestling whatever inner battle he was fighting with himself; and even now, after some considerable time, he still seemed shaken.

"You wanna tell me what happened?" he said, not looking up from where he was deftly sticking together his Rizlas.

Cal was silent for a minute, his head hung between his knees, his unkempt hair all over the place. Then he raised his head and looked out across the dark, empty fields.

"It was me," he said. "I freaked."

"What, 'cause I left you alone?"

"No," Cal replied. "It was Abby and Emma. They were winding me up, I guess. I just couldn't take it. 'Specially not from her."

"Who, Emma?"

"Abby."

"Oh."

After a few moments, Cal took a deep breath and relayed the particulars of their encounter. He hated talking about his shyness, his weakness, and he skipped quickly over the details of how he had become so agitated, concentrating on what Emma and Abby had said and done.

"You know, you might have overreacted," Joel suggested gently. "It might have been genuine."

"Don't *you* start," Cal replied. "Okay, I get Emma caught for smoking and the next day she decides to try and fix me up with one of her friends? What's wrong with this picture? She's just getting her own back."

"So what's Abby got to do with it?"

"Should I know? You know Emma; she' s like . . . the ringleader of everything. Abby's probably just going along with her or something."

"Listen to reason, kid," Joel said. "You fancy her, sure, but is she *good* for you? She's just like the others that hang out with Emma; hair and teeth and make-up, and sod all else."

"I know she is," Cal sighed. Sure, he'd fantasized about how when they met, when they first really *talked*, she'd turn out to be the coolest thing on two legs . . . but realistically, he doubted it. Just looking at who she chose to hang out with, he knew they were incompatible. "She'll just screw me up."

"Probably. Girls are evil, you know. Steer clear of them."

"Like I need to be told *that.* Where were you, anyway?"

Joel finished the construction of the joint, bit off the end and lit it. He took a deep drag, the end of the joint glowing white-red, held it in for a few seconds, and then exhaled. "I was just coming back inside when I met you. I was talking to this guy down that alley that runs by the side of Poppy's. You know, where the fire escape leads out?"

"Right."

"Sorry I was gone so long, I just had some stuff I had to take care of."

"S'alright."

They sat in silence for a while. Cal toked on the joint a bit and felt the relaxing wave of light-headedness spread through him. It did little to make him feel better. They passed it back and forth a couple of times. When it was nearly finished, Cal got to his feet, and Joel rose with him.

The hay-barn that they had been sitting against was only built up on three sides; one side was open to the air to allow the bales to be loaded in and out. Cal sucked the last burn on the joint, and then flicked it into the barn, where it landed in a heap of loose hay at the foot of the bales.

He never knew whether he'd done it on purpose or

not. Had it just been absentmindedness, or had he really subconsciously *wanted* to do what he did? At the time, he wasn't thinking about anything; as soon as the butt had left his fingers it was forgotten.

But where it had hit the hay, thin tendrils of smoke were curling upwards.

"Reckon we'd better get going," Cal murmured.

"You gonna be alright?" Joel asked.

"Yeah, sure," Cal said, waving the question away. "It happens." *But only to me*, he added bitterly to himself. He stooped to lace his boot, which had become undone during the walk.

Joel waited for him. When he was done, he relaced the other one, which had come loose. As Cal was standing up, a scent of something hot and acrid came to Joel. He looked around quizzically, and that was when he saw it.

The hay was on fire. It was tinder-dry, and in a small patch where Cal had flicked the end of the joint, flames were beginning to dance their way free. Thick smoke was churning out from beneath.

"Oh shit, you've set fire to the hay!" Joel cried, running over to the little blaze. He hesitated a moment, then began stamping it, trying to put it out while keeping a wary distance. His efforts just made it worse, scattering the burning hay, spreading the fire. It lapped eagerly at the base of the bales now, multiplying in size with frightening speed. Joel retreated before the cloud of grey smoke and the gathering heat.

Cal had not moved to help. Joel ran up to him.

"Come on! The whole place is gonna burn down. Let's shift it out of here before someone comes!"

Cal did not respond. He was staring into the depths of the barn, where a rim of bright fire was visible beneath the roiling curtain of smoke. There was a distant look on his face. How brilliant it was, how violent in its thrashing . . . and yet so peaceful at its heart, the hot glow deep within. That was where Cal looked, and he felt the anger and the tension and hate draining out of him. It was ascending the bales now; who would have thought it could spread so *quickly*?

"Deaf boy! Are you coming?" Joel urged, tugging his arm.

Cal shook him off, still intent on the fire.

"Listen, do you want to stick around and get blamed for this? I guarantee the farmer who owns this field is gonna be pissed if he catches us!"

"It's beautiful," Cal murmured, just loud enough for Joel to hear.

"No, Cal, it's a *fire*, and we're in it deep if we don't get out of here *now*." He was seriously worried; what was up with Cal?

"You go," Cal said, seeming to snap briefly out of his trance. "I want to stay."

"What? Are you nuts? Come *on*." Joel grabbed his arm and yanked him away, but Cal shook him off again, angrily this time.

"Leave me alone!" he snapped. "I want to stay!"

Joel looked at him in disbelief. He didn't know what else to do. He couldn't *drag* him away. He opened his mouth to say something, and then shut it again.

"Whatever," he said resignedly. "See ya." And with that, he turned and ran.

Cal stood there, transfixed, as the fire became larger, fanned by the wind. After a time, he was forced back by the intensity of the heat. The stacks of bales had become a wall of flame now, collapsing into disarray. Cal watched the way the flames rippled and licked along the blackened hay, and everything else just seemed to fade into wonderful nothingness.

The appearance of the twin lights in the clear dark vaguely registered in Cal's brain. It was only as they got brighter and closer that he realized what they were. Headlights. A car was approaching, or a four-by-four or something. Cal blinked, suddenly realizing where he was.

"Shit," he muttered to himself, and ran.

His feet pounded across the grass, the wind whipping past him as he sprinted for the dirt track and the road beyond. The approaching vehicle – a Range Rover – was coming along the track from the other way. On the far side of the track was a small wooded area.

He crossed the field to the track, but the Rover was too close by now; it would easily outrun him before he reached the road. Instead, he ran across the track, frozen for a moment in the glaring headlights, and plunged into the trees.

Behind him, he heard an exclamation of fury and the sound of the Rover ploughing to a halt, then a door opening and slamming. But he was already buried in the trees, ducking through the moulting branches, pushing them aside as he headed purposefully inwards and away.

It was a few minutes later when Cal emerged from the other edge of the wooded area and back on to the road. The driver hadn't followed him. By the time he had got out of the car, Cal had disappeared.

But he had been seen.

Cal shrugged to himself. It was only for a moment. The driver wouldn't recognize him if he saw him again. Besides, he felt unusually good about himself.

With the memory of the fire still bright in his mind, he turned and began to walk along the yellow-lit streets towards home.

Chapter Four

Fuel

Monday morning was clear, cool and bright, but it had rained during the night and the world was painted in a darker shade of dampness as Abby and Emma rode the bus to school together. The scrubs down at the front of the bus were hollering and scampering about as usual, playing their dumb year-seven games. The bus's engine was labouring steadily in the background as it fought to haul fifty-odd schoolkids up the steep Garrison Way hill, making the windows judder. It was the average noisy chaos of the morning bus ride.

Abby and Emma sat at the back. They were year eleven, so technically there were still two age groups above them who should have taken precedence over the back seat. But the year twelves and thirteens, who were taking their A-levels, thought themselves far too mature to bother themselves with fighting for position on the bus. Their loss, Emma thought.

Abby was sitting with the side of her head leaning on

the glass, feeling the vibrations of the bus hum through her head and rattle her teeth. Emma glanced at her and tutted.

"Bored, are we?" she asked.

"N-n-o-o-o-o," Abby replied, drawing out the word so that the vibrations made her voice jar and wobble with the bumping of the bus. She took her head away from the window. "No, just thinking."

"About what?"

"Friday. Poppy's."

"What about it?" Emma persisted.

"Just . . . I dunno, nothing really," she replied. "Just thinking about it."

Which was a lie. Abby had been thinking about Cal, and about Emma's plan to humiliate him. She felt sort of guilty about what had happened on Friday night. She'd never seen anyone react like Cal did; she'd never seen anyone look so *distressed*. Though she had barely had time to say anything, she surmised that Cal had sussed her and Emma out, and that was why he left. Not just left, really: panicked was more like it. She knew he was a shy kid, but she had no idea. . .

"Speaking of Friday night," Emma said. "What happened with you and Ade, then?" The words were spoken like an accusation.

"*Nothing* happened with me and Ade," Abby replied.

"Yeah, that's what he said. What is *up* with you? He said you were being a real ice queen with him."

"Only 'cause he was trying to paw me all night."

"You know how *long* it took me to try and set that thing up with you and him?" Emma continued, exasperated. "Some thanks."

"I didn't *want* to be fixed up with *anyone*," Abby replied.

Emma sighed, looked out of the window for a moment, then back at Abby.

"Listen," she said. "You're fairly new here, but you're not *that* new. It's kinda getting on for time when you should be going out with someone. Or people are gonna start wondering about you."

Abby was sitting with her arms crossed, listening patiently.

"Ade is *gorgeous*," Emma continued. "It's only 'cause he just broke up with Wendy that I could fix you up at all; I guarantee by now he's got another girlfriend. But if you keep on going like this, turning down all the guys that try it on with you . . . people are gonna think you're a lemon."

Abby waited, but there was nothing more that Emma had to say. "You finished?" she asked.

"Yeah," Emma replied.

"Good," Abby said, then turned and looked out of the window again, ignoring her.

"Oh, you know, you are *so* ungrateful," Emma said. "I don't know why I waste my time with you."

"Waste your *time*?" Abby exclaimed, aghast. "Listen, I'm not one of your *projects*, Emma. The boys you try and fix me up with are all the same: they just want to get you in the sack and be over with it."

"So what's wrong with that? It's as good a place to

start a relationship as any!" Emma replied. "A better place than most, in fact," she added languorously.

"Yeah, well, it's not my style, okay? Can we leave it now? And I'd like it if you didn't try to fix me up again with any of your friends. I'll pick my own, if that's okay with you."

"Fine," Emma replied, shrugging. "You do whatever."

"I will, thanks," Abby said.

Emma arched an eyebrow and was silent.

The bus pulled into the lay-by outside the school and burped out squealing clots of children on to the pavement. The older years followed, walking out with a little more self-respect. Abby and Emma came last, sauntering down the drive to the school like they owned the place, and everyone else was here on their sufferance.

"You didn't give it much of a try on Friday night with Cal," Emma commented out of nowhere, breaking the silence.

"I didn't get much of a chance," Abby replied. "You must have been laying it on with a trowel about how I was supposed to fancy him. He had me figured almost straight away."

Emma shrugged. "I thought I was being pretty subtle, myself."

"Maybe he's a little smarter than you thought," Abby said, kicking a stone.

"It doesn't matter how smart he is," Emma said with a toss of her blonde ringlets. "Guys have this override system which makes them ignore what their brain is telling them. You just have to appeal to the right organ."

"Oh, you are *sick*," Abby said, laughing.

"Believe me, I speak from long experience. Right now, even though Cal's head is telling him that we're just playing around with him, there's this liiiitle voice that's saying that maybe, just maybe, he's in with a chance. He'll crack. We just have to keep at him."

Abby looked unenthusiastic. "Come on now, like, I think we've done enough. You didn't see his face when he ran. It was—"

"That's not *enough*," Emma crowed. "We haven't even started. But you've got to go and find him today, okay? 'Cause you blew it on Friday. It's your turn."

"Yeah. I guess so," Abby said.

"Good. I'll expect a full report on the bus on the way back." Emma smiled mischievously, kissed Abby on the cheek and then said: "I gotta go meet Rob before class. See ya!" And then she hurried away towards the steps behind the technology department, where her boyfriend would be waiting.

Abby sighed. She'd thought it was funny at first, this whole idea about Cal. But now it just seemed nasty. She wasn't *that* bothered about being beaten in the art comp, and certainly not enough to hold a grudge about it. She wished Emma would let it drop. But that wasn't something that would easily happen. And while Emma was still up for it, she had to go along with the plan.

Am I really this shallow? she thought to herself.

Feeling a little depressed, she shouldered her bag and trudged to class.

The dark green Peugeot 405 pulled up before the

cluster of police vehicles that were parked haphazardly across the dirt track. Ben Deerborn reached to shut off the radio before killing the engine. He still wasn't familiar with all the bits and bobs on this car, and he had a tendency to leave the radio on loud when he turned off the ignition, so that when he turned it on again later he jumped out of his skin as some American soul diva howled deafeningly in his ear.

I got you this time, he thought to himself, stabbing the power button before getting out.

Deerborn was a tall man, wide-shouldered and wearing a long beige trenchcoat. He had a full-face beard and short, wiry black hair that framed eyes of deep brown, eyes that were more than a little reddened and bloodshot. The fine tracery of red veins that cracked the edges of his eyeballs stood out uncomfortably against his dark brown skin.

Rolling his shoulders and massaging the back of his neck with one big hand, he walked through the mud towards the cluster of people in the field. Last night's rain had churned it up badly, and by the time he reached the grass it had made a grimy tidemark on his shoes. He didn't care.

"So what's the story, Mike?" he said as he approached a balding officer in his late forties who was talking to an irate farmer.

"Oh, hi, Ben," he said, glancing at him.

"And if you'd bin here on Saturday mornin', when I called you, maybe you *would* be able to tell us somethin'!" said the farmer, continuing the tirade that Ben had interrupted.

"Mr Watkins, this is Ben Deerborn, our arson specialist," said Mike. "I'm sure that now he's here, we can find out what happened."

"If you'd've come when I phoned, there'd still have been some footprints in that mucky trail out there," Mr Watkins pointed out sullenly. "Bloody rain's washed 'em all away by now."

"We *have* been very busy, sir," Mike said.

"Not busy enough," Mr Watkins muttered, stomping away.

Deerborn and Mike exchanged glances.

"Didn't expect you back with us for a while yet," Mike said. "I know you don't want to hear this, but I'd feel bad if I didn't say it. I'm really sorry about what happened, Ben. We all are."

"Thanks," said Ben. "That means a lot. So tell me what happened here."

Mike led him over to where a sodden heap of incinerated hay and wood spread across the field like a bruise. "This fella's hay-barn burned down. Says he saw a kid running away from the fire. Thinks it was started on purpose. We were going to look it over, but then I know you don't like anything touched, so we left it for you." Mike frowned at him, looking into his haggard face and bloodshot eyes. "Are you sure you're alright?"

"No, I'm not alright," Deerborn replied quietly. "But I'd rather be at work where I have something to keep my mind off it."

Mike knew the "it" that he was talking about. He nodded.

"Let's get on, then," Deerborn said, pulling on a set of rubber gloves.

He crossed over to the heap of wet debris and squatted down on his haunches, then began slowly, methodically, looking for clues and signs. Traces of petrol burn, a blast pattern where a container of kerosene might have been used, a clue as to the source of ignition, something that would tell him whether this was done on purpose, accidentally, or if the fire had been natural.

As he searched, his mind began to wander. It had been happening to him a lot since the accident. He seemed to be unable to stop his mind from straying back to his wife and son, as if they were magnets, pulling his thoughts steadily and constantly. He pictured their faces, heard their voices, felt them laugh and cry again. And he felt again the aching stab of guilt and pain as he remembered that he was the one responsible for their deaths.

It was something so small, the tiniest moment in time. A wet road, a sharp corner in the dark, and maybe he hadn't been paying enough attention because he was leaning over to say something to Carl, his son; but he hadn't been able to hold the turn, and the car had fishtailed into a tree, and his wife and son had been killed. His fault.

And he could never forgive himself for it.

He caught himself. This was his first day back at work since the accident. It wouldn't do him any good to think about them here. Resolutely, he pushed them away to the back of his mind and concentrated on the job at hand.

He found the roach-end of the joint after a few minutes. What puzzled him about it was the fact that it was there at all. It should have been destroyed in the blaze. He guessed that it was either thrown clear somehow – perhaps by someone trying to kick out the fire – or that it was not this that started the fire. Either way, it didn't make it look particularly intentional. It was too crisped to provide any fingerprints, but he bagged it anyway.

The search took him a good hour, but he found no other signs. Eventually, he returned to where Mike and Mr Watkins – the owner of the barn, he guessed – were waiting, filling out report forms.

"Find anything?" Mike asked, as he approached.

"Roach end," he replied.

"What do you think?"

"There's not any real evidence either way. This could've been dropped here any time over the last week, or even before that. I think it'd be best if we talked to the kid that Mr Watkins saw."

Mike scratched behind his ear with the butt of his pen. "Well, unfortunately Mr Watkins has not been able to come up with much of a description on this lad."

"It were dark," Mr Watkins protested. "He only ran across me 'eadlights for a second."

"So what *do* we have?" Deerborn asked his colleague.

"Not very tall, hair sort of thatchy and all over the place, wearing jeans and some kind of black top."

"That doesn't do us a lot of good," he commented.

"Well, if you'd have bin here when I *called*—" Mr Watkins began, but Deerborn cut him off.

"We've heard enough of that one, sir."

Deerborn stood there for a few moments, thinking; then he appeared to reach a decision.

"Well, as far as this preliminary investigation goes, I can't tell you anything for sure. I'll get this roach analysed, but I'm ninety-nine per cent sure that it's too toasted to be of any value. As to your barn, sir," he said, addressing Mr Watkins, "I'm sure you have insurance. We'll do our best to find this kid; but beyond that, this doesn't look very hopeful. Even if we caught him, there's not enough evidence to do anything so far."

"So you're gonna let 'im get away with it?" Mr Watkins demanded.

"No, sir. But there is very little we can do. I suggest you contact your insurance company for compensation. Good morning."

Deerborn turned away then, leaving Mike to pacify the farmer. He wasn't in the mood to sugar-coat it for anyone today. He felt bleak and bitter, and he had other things on his mind.

Abby made her excuses and left the group of girls that had gathered around Emma behind the walls of the bike sheds. Contrary to the cliché, the bike sheds at Bishop Grove were the last place that anyone would go to get off with somebody; they were far too open and visible. But of course, visibility was what Emma wanted. She loved to be seen, especially with her knot of cronies around her.

Abby crunched on a red apple as she wandered

around the front of the school, heading towards the car park and from there to the back of the science block. She had adopted the resigned attitude of somebody forced to do an unpleasant chore. Of course, nobody was actually *forcing* her, but it was sort of something she had to do. She knew what Emma was like; if she didn't follow through with this, Emma would freeze her out, and then where would she be? If Emma didn't like someone, her gang followed suit. Abby didn't much fancy being friendless.

Some friends, girl, she thought to herself. But what could she do about it? Nothing.

She kept on replaying that moment in her head when Cal had run from her, the moment of realization on his face. She couldn't stop thinking about it. It made her sick with shame to remember the raw hurt in his expression. And now here she was, doing it again.

She bit deep into her apple. This wasn't right, and she knew that. She just didn't have the strength to stand up to Emma and tell her so.

The corner to the back of the science block neared. She hesitated for a moment, took a breath, brushed her hair behind her ear, and turned the corner.

Cal was there, as he always was, sitting on the steps at an angle, one knee higher than the other, reading a book and eating slices of what looked like pizza from a Tupperware box.

She stopped. The sight of him provoked a sudden flood of pity in her chest. He was here almost every lunchtime, by all accounts. Not talking to anyone, not seeing anyone, staying out of people's way. Suddenly, for some reason, she felt so bad for him that she almost gave up her mission altogether.

Instead of approaching him immediately, she leaned against the wall, ate her apple, and watched him. Something about him interested her. Maybe it was how peaceful he looked while he was reading. She didn't know why, but for a time she was content to just watch him buried in his novel.

Then he looked up, glanced around, and saw her. She could almost feel him reddening as he avoided her gaze, riveting his attention back on the book in his hands, trying to be invisible, pretending he hadn't noticed her.

And as she tossed the core of her apple into the bushes and walked over to talk to him, it was half because Emma was making her do it and half because she wanted to. She was curious. She wanted to know who this guy was.

"Hey," she said as she stood before him, resting her weight on one leg.

Cal muttered something in reply, barely glancing up from the book.

"How's it going?"

She thought he said "Okay," but it was almost whispered and she couldn't be sure. His face was burning red.

"You know, you left pretty early on Friday night," she said.

"Uh-huh."

Abby sighed, squatting down in front of him. "What, you hate me so much that you won't even look at me?"

"No," he said, sounding as if he was struggling for breath. "S'not it."

She looked at his face. He was sweating. This kid must have something badly wrong with him, she thought.

"What's on the pizza?" she asked, struggling to find a foothold to talk with him.

"Chocolate and banana," he said, the words coming out in a rush.

She smiled. "Sweet tooth, huh?"

"Yeah," he mumbled.

"Listen, I—" she began, but she was suddenly and unexpectedly cut off when Cal looked up, his face an expression of rage.

"Alright, *stop* it, okay?" he shouted, making her jump. "You and Emma. You had your fun, okay. You got your kicks. Now leave me the hell alone, alright? Why don't you just leave me *alone*?"

Abby was momentarily so shocked that she didn't respond.

"I didn't even *do* anything to you," he said, his voice dropping to a choked whisper again. And then he scooped up his stuff, shoved it in his bag and ran, through the car park and away, heading towards the main road out of school.

Abby sat down where he had been sitting on the steps. She brushed her hair behind her ear and took a deep breath. She couldn't remember ever feeling as much of a scumbag as she did right then.

Chapter Five

Flashpoint

"Cal?"

Joel let the letterbox snap shut and knocked on the door again. Once more, there was no reply.

He stood there, in front of the large brown rough-stone detached house that Cal had all to himself during the week. It was beginning to get dim even at this hour, barely six o'clock, and the sun was descending slowly behind the trellis fence of the nearby park. After a few moments, he went over to the gate that led around the side of the house. It was unlocked. He lifted the latch and went on through to the back garden.

Cal was there, kneeling with his back to the house. In front of him was a wire shopping basket, packed full of paper and wood and burning fiercely. It was propped up on a couple of bricks to let the air get underneath it.

Joel's forehead crinkled in concern. He was beginning to get severely worried about his friend's obsession with fire. He could still remember the glazed look on Cal's face when they'd stood in front of that burning barn. Quietly, he opened the gate and walked closer.

Cal was rocking gently back and forth, staring into the fire. This time, he didn't seem to have that blank expression like before; instead, his eyes darted around the flames, as if searching for something that he was unable to find. He held a mug of coffee in his hands.

"Cal," he said.

Cal turned around, his gaze finding his friend.

"What?" he said.

"Uhh . . . what are you doing?" Joel asked, motioning with his hand at the blazing basket.

Cal seemed to mentally shake himself. "Nothing. It doesn't matter. It doesn't work now anyway. Come inside."

"Hang on. What doesn't work?" Joel persisted as Cal got to his feet.

"I *said*, it doesn't matter," Cal replied, with a slightly threatening edge in his voice that Joel had never heard before.

"O*kay*, just asking," Joel said under his breath as Cal stalked inside.

They went into the living room, which was all set out in cosy beige and white. Cal ignored the plush sofas and sat cross-legged on the floor, sipping his coffee. Joel sank into one of the armchairs and pulled out a tobacco tin from his pocket that was packed full of all the essentials for rolling a joint.

"I worry about you," he said, as he drew the papers out and began sticking them together. "Dunno why, but I do."

"What, 'cause of the caffeine?"

"No, the other stuff."

"Yeah, well," Cal replied neutrally, his knuckles draped on the carpet and his head hung.

"Didn't see you in class this afternoon," Joel said. "Figured you'd gone home early. Something happen?"

"Abby and Emma," Cal said, shrugging. "They won't quit."

"Want me to say something to them?"

"No."

"Alright."

Cal paused. "I gave Abby a mouthful today," he said. "Maybe she'll leave me alone now."

"I thought you sorta liked her?" Joel asked, looking up from where he was packing the paper with tobacco.

"I did. I *do*. I held back on her." He scratched at his laces. "Shit, this sucks. Why do I still like her? She's such a *bitch*. She's just like all the other girls who hang out with Emma."

Joel agreed heartily on this point. He and Abby had never got along. He had a predisposition to hate all of Emma's gang – her included – and he didn't make much of a secret of it. As Cal had just said, he thought they were all the same: snide, insufferable girls who thought they were better than everyone else. Near the start of the year, he'd been watching his then-girlfriend Caroline in the tryouts for the drama club production of *A Streetcar Named Desire*. When Abby had come on, he'd laughed at her out of spite, even though she was actually quite good. But she'd got her own back, by beating Caroline to the lead role of Blanche, condemning Joel to a fortnight of listening to his girl-friend whine about the unfairness of it all.

It wasn't the ideal way to foster a friendship; and it got worse after that. After that first incident, each seemed to go out of their way to antagonize the other, for no reason that either of them could guess at. Joel theorized that ninety per cent of school relationships were based on motives equally as pointless and random. Knowing this didn't stop him participating, however; and over the few months that Abby had been at Bishop Grove, she and Joel had developed quite a distaste for each other.

"You know, if you want them to leave you alone, you can't just avoid them," he advised. "Give 'em shit. You've gotta stand up to them."

Cal sighed. "I know. It's not as easy as that."

Joel glanced at him. "Yeah, I guess. Hey, you took the bandages off your hand."

"It's pretty much healed now," Cal said.

"You must have cracked it bad when you dropped that kettle on it."

"Bastard thing about broke my knuckles," Cal said, smiling faintly.

Joel put down the half-constructed joint. "You told me that someone slammed a door on it," he said gravely.

Cal was silent.

"Punched a wall?" Joel asked, knowing full well the answer.

"Something like that," he admitted. "Anyway, what the hell do you care?"

"Here it comes again, the martyr bit," Joel said. "God, you think I'd put up with all your crap if I *didn't* care?"

Cal glared at him, eyes blazing, but then the heat went out of him. "Reckon not."

"You gotta get some help, Cal," Joel said, leaning forward. "This thing with the fires, I don't like it."

Cal avoided his eyes. "You don't have to like it," he said. "It helps calm me down. When stuff gets on top of me. Saves punching the hell out of myself, anyway."

There was a knock at the door.

"To be continued," Joel said, his face serious.

"Maybe," Cal replied, getting up to answer the door.

Standing on his doorstep were a group of three lads, about twenty or so, dressed in puffer jackets. Cal thought he recognized one of them from the group of guys Joel hung out with down at the track, behind the school. He was a half-caste, with blunt little dreadlocks.

"Joel here?" asked the nearest one, who was wearing a bright gold earring.

"Yeah," Cal replied.

The next thing he knew was that he was being shoved roughly out of the way as the three lads piled into his hallway and strode purposefully through it. He cried out in surprise, but they paid him no attention. In a few moments, they had disappeared into the living room, leaving the front door open.

"Alright, Joel," came a voice from the living room. "Didn't expect to see us, did you? We tried your house, and your mum was kind enough to tell us where you were."

Cal hurried back to the living-room door and peered through. The three lads were facing Joel, who had also got up. He could feel the crushing onset of that familiar feeling again, making him panicky and short of breath. What did they want? Were they friends or enemies?

But from their cold expressions, and Joel's guarded posture, he knew the answer to that one.

"Listen, right, I don't have it all yet," Joel was saying, glancing nervously at each of them. "I've been trying to shift that stuff, but no one wants to buy. It's dud."

Earring looked down at his feet and then back up at Joel and sighed. It was a kind of *I'm sorry I have to do this but* . . . gesture that Cal didn't like.

"It's a matter of reputation, Joel," he said. "I've already given you more time than I should have, but that's because I knew you were gonna have a hard time selling that stuff once it got out that it was a dud batch. I can't give you any more time. If I let *you* have some slack, I've got to let everyone *else* have some slack, and it just doesn't *work* like that."

"But I can pay you what I owe!" Joel replied, his voice scared. "I can! Just give me till Friday night. I'll find someone who'll buy."

"Sorry, man," Earring said. "No exceptions."

With that, he swung a punch hard into Joel's stomach. Joel gasped and went down, retching. A moment later, they were all over him, raining blows down, laying into him with kicks. He was all curled up, his arms over his face, trying to protect himself; but they were hitting him from all sides, a constant barrage.

Cal was frozen. He couldn't believe what he was

seeing. In his own *house*? His best (and only) friend was getting a kicking in his own *house*? He couldn't just stand by and watch this! But what could he do? He was trembling, paralysed, his face and body throbbing and tingling. And all the while, before his eyes, his friend was being beaten.

Do something! he begged himself, but his body would not respond. *Do anything!*

And then there was a sickening thud, a particularly vicious kick into Joel's thigh, and he couldn't stop himself from yelling in pain that time; and that yell was too much for Cal. Suddenly he was moving, stumbling up the stairs towards his bedroom, doors passing him by unnoticed on either side of the corridor. His own door was at the end, plastered with stickers and dominated by the big plastic "BIOHAZARD" warning sign. He threw it open, rushing into his room, skidding to his knees at the foot of his bed. Frantically he reached underneath, pawing around among the junk that was piled there; and then his hand closed on cold metal, and he knew he had found what he was looking for.

He ran back along the corridor and down the stairs, the terrible hot, choking feeling of his fear forgotten in the chill wash of adrenalin. He reached the doorway of the living room. They still hadn't let up yet, circling Joel like jackals, occasionally offering a swift kick or punch to an exposed part of his body.

"Hey!" Cal cried, and he was surprised by how loud his voice was. They turned to look at him as one, standing in the doorway; and they froze when they saw him.

Clasped in his grip, one hand folded over the other, he held a Colt .45 pointed at them.

"Get the hell out of my house," he said, his voice trembling.

The lads paused, a moment of indecision; then Earring smirked. "What you gonna do, kill us?" he said.

"No. Kneecaps," Cal replied, and he lowered the barrel of the gun to emphasize his point, swallowing against a throat that had gone desert-dry.

The lads were maintaining an outward calm, pretending they weren't intimidated; but Cal could tell that they were unnerved by this sudden turn of events. He held the gaze of Earring, who was clearly the leader. He was staring back, trying to decide if Cal was bluffing or not.

After a moment, he shrugged. "Okay, let's get out of here. We're done anyhow."

Cal moved aside to make room for them as they came out of his living room and into the hall, staying at a distance so they couldn't make a grab for him. They walked past, staring hatefully at Cal, leaving Joel huddled on the floor, and went out of the front door.

Earring was the last to go. Before he left, he stopped and turned around, looking at Cal levelly. "Tell Joel he's got till Friday to come up with the money, or he gets more of the same. And you, you little bastard . . . you are *dead meat* when I see you next."

Turning, he walked away as casually as he could. Cal shut the door behind him. Slowly, he sat down with his back against the hallway wall, put the gun aside, and hugged his knees. He began shaking, trembling so badly that it rattled his teeth.

It took him almost five minutes before he had recovered enough to return to the lounge. When he did, he found Joel sitting back in his chair, smoking the joint he had been constructing before the lads had turned up. He had an awesome bruise on one eye, and the tip of his cheekbone was a taut purple. He looked awful.

Cal walked past him and poured a mug of coffee out of the percolator. He put it down next to Joel, then repossessed his spot on the floor and drank his own. After a while, Joel passed him the joint. He toked it down, feeling the hot smoke billow into his lungs, the spread of airiness flooding through his body.

"Thanks," Joel said through swollen lips.

"S'alright," Cal replied. "How you feeling?"

"I think it hurts more when they stop kicking you," he said thoughtfully. "You sorta don't feel it at the time."

Cal took a drag and blew it out, filling the room with the pungent aroma of draw.

"Where d'you get the gun?" Joel asked after a time.

"S'not a *real* gun," Cal said. "Replica. I don't think you can even get Colts in this country anyway."

Joel smiled and winced as his bruised face protested at the movement. "Fooled me," he said. "And them."

"It's supposed to," Cal said.

There was silence again. Cal took a long burn on the joint and blew out, the smoke turning from a jet to a cloud and feathering away.

"So you wanna tell me who they were?" Cal said.

Joel took a heavy breath. "The guy with the earring

is called Sully. He's like, this dealer guy. Deals in all sorts."

"Draw, right?"

"Yeah, draw. Among other things. So anyway, this guy I sometimes see down the track—"

"The guy with the little dreads?"

"Yeah, him. Weldon. He sorta got to telling me about how he made all this money dealing draw, how he got it off this local supplier called Sully. Said it was easy money, you could do it on your nights out, and you always had a supply for yourself."

"So you started dealing," Cal said.

"Just to people I know. Small scale, right? Didn't want to be responsible for anyone I couldn't keep an eye on and stop selling to if I thought they were getting stupid. Most of the stuff we've had recently has been mine."

"How long you been doing it, then?"

"I've been doing it for months," Joel replied.

"Oh," Cal said, a little noise that conveyed a lot. He took a toke.

Joel sighed. "Last time I met him, I got a big block off him. Thing is, I'd kinda spent most of the money I had, so he gave it to me on credit. Said I could sell it at whatever price I wanted, pay him and keep the profit." He touched the side of his face delicately, probing the soreness. "But it was a dud batch. Fake stuff, or maybe it just didn't have any kick in it, I don't know. Either way, I wouldn't sell it to the guys I knew, 'cause I didn't want to rip them off. So I flogged it to strangers. The first few people I sold it off to were, like, less than satisfied."

78

"Was that who those guys who chased us were? When I about got run over by that train?" Cal's voice was flat and emotionless now.

"Yeah," Joel said. "I'd sold some to them. They remembered me."

"And that's where you went off to on Friday night, when you disappeared for so long. Down that alley, you were trying to sell some off, weren't you?"

Joel shrugged, looking at his hands. "Yeah. But word's spread by now. Nobody's gonna buy off me now they know I'm selling fake stuff."

"And unless you can sell it, you can't pay Sully back."

"Right."

Cal finished off the remainder of the joint. He stubbed it out in an ashtray, then looked up at Joel.

"What I don't get about all this," Cal said, "is why didn't you tell me anything?"

Joel didn't answer.

"I mean, you've been doing this for months? And you never said a word about it to me? That's not an oversight; you did that on purpose."

Still Joel didn't respond. He looked at the palms of his hands and flexed them.

"I know what this is," said Cal, easing himself to his feet because his legs were still a little shaky. "You've got your cool friends, and you've got me. And the two don't mix, right? That's fair enough. But why didn't you tell me, huh? How long have we known each other? How much other stuff don't you tell me about?"

"God, Cal, you're not my *girlfriend*," Joel said

quietly. "It's not like I'm going behind your back or any-thing."

Cal looked at him for a moment in disbelief, then slowly shook his head and smiled bitterly. "No. Heh. No, you don't get it, do you?" He turned away. "I'm going out."

"Uh?" Joel said quizzically.

"I'm just going, okay?" he said, walking out of the living room. A few moments later, the front door slammed.

Joel sat alone in the living room of his friend's house and stared into space. His face and body ached with bruises. After a time, he gathered up his stuff, got up from his chair and went home, leaving the front door unlocked behind him.

Pan Adams woke up. It was cold on his face, but he was wrapped up in layers of clothing and blankets, and his body was caked in stale sweat. The air was filled with a sharp and acrid scent that seemed to burn his nose and wrap around his tongue. He knew immedi-ately that something was wrong. Sitting up in his makeshift nest, he looked around.

The dark back room of the disused factory was empty and uncluttered, the moonlight from outside falling on a bare stone floor. He'd cleared it out when he'd discovered this place: a small building, right on the river bank and opposite the textile mill. Nobody else had found it yet, as far as he knew. It was his own place. Sure, it was draughty, and the stone floor became unbearably cold during some of the autumn nights; but it was his own, and he didn't have to share it with anyone.

But that smell was getting to him. He knew it, but he couldn't quite place it. It wasn't natural gas, or oil, or anything like that. It was something from out of his past, something that went all the way back to the time when he wasn't homeless, but he was living out of a caravan with his hippy parents. The ones who had given him such a stupid hippy name, after the mythical satyr that played pipes and made people crazy.

There had been this time when he'd been running around the caravan playing with his planes. He'd tripped over a plastic container and knocked the top off, spilling the liquid all over the floor, and suddenly the air had filled with this smell. The same smell that filled the air now.

Paraffin. Or what did they call it now, the American name, because everything was going American these days?

Kerosene.

Pan scrambled out of his blankets and got to his feet. What the hell was going on?

He walked across to the empty doorway that led on to the main floor of the factory. He had come to the conclusion that the place couldn't have been abandoned for long because there was very little rubble or litter about, except where the little squared windows had been smashed in by kids. He'd always suspected that there might be a reason why nobody else came here, something that he didn't know about. For a moment, he was seized with the fear that he might find out what that reason was.

In the middle of the factory floor, six or seven big plastic containers were standing together in a loose circle around a metal gas canister. The faint moonlight limned their edges. A heap of rags was stuffed in between them, and a glistening trail of what might have been petrol led away from them and under the closed door that led on to the riverside path. The canister was hissing with the sound of escaping gas.

Eyes widening in horror, Pan turned and fled, suddenly knowing what must be coming next. As he ran into the back room, he could almost feel the flame rushing along the trail of petrol, ignited from some distance away. At any moment, it would hit the petrol-soaked rags, but before it even got there, it would probably set off the kerosene and incinerate the place. . .

He scrambled through the window of the back room, his bolthole for emergencies. Emergencies like this. Dropping to the grassy, uneven ground behind the factory, he made a run for it, but he hadn't gone two steps before he was jerked off his feet and roughly slammed back against the wall beneath the frame. Momentarily dazed, he flailed helplessly for a few seconds before realizing what had happened. The tail of his long coat had snagged a protruding bit of the window frame.

Scrambling to his feet, aware that every second was precious, he tore it loose and ran. His battered boots dug into mushy grass and dirt as he raced uphill for the safety of the distant line of trees.

Come on, please, don't blow up yet, just a few more seconds, just a few more.

If anyone heard his silent plea, they chose to take it literally. A few seconds later, the gas and kerosene ignited with a dull *WHOOMPH* that belched tongues of flame from the windows of the little factory. He was still too close. The shockwave of superheated air curled the hair on the back of his neck a moment before the flame rolled out to consume him . . . and though he did not see it, fell short by mere inches before blowing itself out and disappearing back into the factory.

He leaped forward at the same moment, crashing into the turf, unsure whether he was dead or alive. Behind him, he could hear the crackling as the roof timbers of the factory began to burn. For long seconds, he lay face down, just breathing. Then he became aware of a painful sensation on the back of his legs, gathering swiftly in intensity until it became suddenly unbearable. Jerking up, he looked over his shoulder.

Shit, I'm on fire!

The tail of his long coat was burning, the flame crawling up his legs towards his back. Frantically, he stood up and shucked his coat off his shoulders, desperate to be away from the blazing agony. He threw it aside, and the pain diminished instantly, becoming instead a patch of stinging soreness on his calves where he had been burned. Mercifully, his trousers had not caught fire.

The factory was burning well now. Mostly it was the wooden underside of the roof that was feeding the flames, but the explosion seemed to have caught on to other things too, even crisping the damp grass that surrounded the building on three sides. The dark night bathed in the dancing light of the blaze, weaving along the rippling edges of the black river water, throwing its warm glow everywhere.

Pan was still breathing hard from his close escape. He didn't want to move yet. He watched the factory burn, his home for a short time. He watched the fire eating his coat near by. And then his eyes fell on something else. A kid, maybe fifteen or sixteen, standing at the edge of the fire's light, watching with him. Pan stared at him for a time. Was it *him* who'd done it? *Why?*

He was about to go down there and get that kid, find out what he knew; but at that moment the distant howl of a fire engine drifted to them over the hum of the town. The kid looked around once like a frightened animal and then ran back into the darkness.

Pan watched him go. He would remember that kid.

Chapter Six

Flame

Cal didn't walk to school with Joel on Tuesday. He loaded up on coffee as soon as he fell out of the shower, then left the house fifteen minutes before Joel usually called. He chose a long and winding route that took him around the more scenic areas of town before arriving at Bishop Grove via the small gate at the side. He didn't feel like talking to Joel today.

Joel just didn't understand. For months, Cal had watched him disappearing off with his other friends, hanging out with the cool crowd at school. That didn't bother Cal; he would have felt worse if Joel had felt obligated to hang around with him on their own. It didn't bother him, because no matter what Joel did at school, they were still good friends. They went around to each other's house a lot. They saw each other on weekends. They'd grown up together, largely under the same roof, so close they were practically brothers.

And they'd always trusted each other. They'd always told each other everything.

Cal was angry. Joel had kept something from him; a *big* something. What, did he think he was too fragile to take it? Did he think that it would send his weird friend over the edge?

The thing was, Joel knew enough to realize that Cal wouldn't be bothered about him being a dealer. He wouldn't even be particularly *against* it, as long as he only dealt in the soft stuff, and only to his friends. He'd have just told him to be careful.

What was really bugging him, though, was that it just seemed like the beginning of the end. Joel had been spending less and less time with him. It started at school, when he would wander off to see his other friends more and more frequently. But more recently, it had spread to after-school hours as well. Joel called less often. He was hardly ever in. They rarely did anything on weekends any more.

Cal knew he was a drag, he knew he was unexciting; but it wasn't his fault. It was this damn problem that he had with his head that made him so antisocial.

And now he felt he was losing the only friend he had.

"Getting angry with him is *not* gonna help your cause, dumbass," he muttered to himself as he walked up the narrow side-drive towards the school. But he couldn't help it. And he knew that.

The morning passed by around him, as it usually did. He went to maths, sat on his own, and drew doodles in his book while the teacher waffled in a depressing monotone. He skived history, because he knew Joel would be there, and finished the Orson Scott Card book he'd been reading. After that, he wandered down into town to the nearby library, returned the book and got a new one out.

When he came back, it was midway through lunch break. He took a route through the school so he wouldn't have to pass by the place where Joel would be hanging. The corridors were still fairly busy, and he walked with his head down and his hands thrust in his pockets, hurrying to his spot on the science block steps where he could be alone.

"Hey, Cal!" called out a voice suddenly, and his heart sank. Emma Cobley. Come to torment him some more, no doubt.

He stopped anyway, waiting for her to catch up with him.

"You know, you are a hard man to find," she said, stopping next to him. She ran her hand through her blonde ringlets, and smiled cutely, looking slightly flushed from her run. Was she ever gorgeous, Cal couldn't help thinking.

"I was out," he said. This time, the shyness didn't seem to have so much of a grip on him. Maybe he was getting used to Emma, or maybe it was because he was still angry at Joel. Maybe it was because he'd managed to push down the fear last night to face those lads in his house. For whatever reason, though, this time he at least seemed to retain the power of speech.

"Out where? You were skiving?" Emma's eyes flashed in false admiration. "You never struck me as the type."

Cal shrugged.

"Abby said you had a go at her yesterday," Emma said.

"She deserved it," Cal said. Then he looked at her and added: "So do you."

"You know, you are *really* hard to like," she replied. "I mean, you make it really hard for someone to like you. Why are you so mean?"

"Why are you messing around with me?" Cal countered, the question put bluntly.

"You think that, don't you? You think me and Abby are playing a game with you or something."

Cal looked sceptical. "Now you're gonna tell me you aren't?"

"No," she frowned. "I mean yes. I am going to tell you that. That we're not playing with you." She looked confused for a second. "Or something."

"So what's the real story?" Cal asked. He knew he was going to disbelieve whatever she said, but he was strangely curious as well.

"What, is it so hard to believe? I mean, I suppose we can talk openly about it now, 'cause you seem to know. What's so unbelievable about two girls fancying the same guy? We do it all the *time.* Girls are always falling out because they fancy the same guy. It's, like, natural."

"Two girls," Cal replied. "Uh-huh. You and Abby, right?"

Emma looked coy. "Well . . . yeah."

Cal smiled sarcastically. "Yeah. Sincerely."

"It was like this thing we did, like 'may the best girl win'," Emma said, looking at him earnestly. "I'd try and fix you up with her, and she'd try and fix you up with me. Thing is, she hasn't been trying very hard, so I kinda thought I'd jump the gun a bit."

Cal was no longer aware of the people bustling by, the hollow squeak of their shoes on the polished floors of the corridor. Right now, his whole being was focused on the slim and beautiful shape of Emma Cobley. And no matter how much he protested his disbelief, something was saying to him: *Don't throw away this chance!* Emma's explanation seemed to make sense of her and Abby's bizarre behaviour, and if he could accept that the girls really did like him – and it wasn't *that* much of a leap of faith, stranger things have happened – then wasn't it possible that what Emma was saying was true? Every dog has his day, right? Could this be his? Could he live with himself if he missed it because he was too cynical and paranoid?

"You don't fancy me," he said, trying to persuade himself more than her. "You never even talked to me before Friday."

"You're not an easy person to approach," Emma said. "Come on, how am I supposed to talk to you? Just walk up and say hi?"

"You could," he replied quietly.

"I *did*, in case you don't remember. In Poppy's? And how did you react then?"

There was a pause. "So what about Rob?" Cal said. He hated himself for saying it. He was actually getting sucked into her story. It wasn't that he believed her, it was that he *wanted* to believe her so badly.

"Rob's a pain. He and I are gonna be history soon,"

she replied. She began to smile seductively. "So what about it?"

"What about what?"

She took his hands, looked down at them bashfully, swinging their linked arms gently between their bodies. "What about, like, you and me?"

Cal almost died on the spot. "You and me?" he managed to mumble.

"You know, going out?"

"Uhh. . ." he said. His brain had shifted into neutral, and was freewheeling over the shock.

"God, I'm *asking* you, okay? You want me to throw myself at your feet or something?"

"Yes," he said. Emma stared at him in disbelief. "I mean, yes I will," he managed to say after a second.

Emma's features softened. Still holding his hands, she said: "Give me a kiss, then. To seal it."

Cal's heart was thumping, but this time it was a *good* thing. An exciting thing. And he was flushed, but this time it was because he couldn't believe what was happening. Here, in the middle of the school corridor, he was going to kiss Emma Cobley. The most beautiful girl in the school.

He had never kissed a girl before. And now he was going to kiss *the* girl.

A faint picture of Rob flashed through his mind. Screw Rob. If he only got *one* kiss off this girl, it would be worth all the pain that Rob could dish out.

She closed her eyes and leaned towards him. He closed his eyes and leaned towards her. He could feel the tiniest flutter of her breath on his lips.

And then, when their lips had almost touched, she slid away from him.

"Ewww, as *if*!" she cried, an expression of disgust on her face.

Around him, the corridor exploded in laughter; and it was then that he realized that people had stopped in curiosity when they saw Emma Cobley holding hands with this unknown kid, and they had been witness to his humiliation.

Oh, God, no! he thought. It *had* been a trick all along. He knew it! He knew it but he didn't *listen* to himself! He felt his throat close up, felt himself swamped with embarrassment, looking around at the faces that were laughing at him and back to Emma, who was laughing too.

"Did you *actually* think I'd *go* with you? Come on, freak boy, who do you think you're dealing with?"

He couldn't breathe. Couldn't answer. Couldn't even run, to get away from this nightmare back to safety. He was trapped.

"I knew you'd believe me, you sucker," she continued, crowing. "You guys can only think with one part of you."

And then suddenly the heat and hate trapped in Cal had to find a way out, had to be vented on something. He couldn't bear the humiliation any more. So he lashed out. It was the only way.

"Yeah, and you'd *know* about that one part, wouldn't you?" he suddenly shouted, and his voice was loud and angry enough to make the laughter die rapidly.

"What?" Emma replied, a little shocked at his response.

"Well, come on, let's not beat around the bush here, you never got to where you are by merit, did you? You slept your way to the top."

"*What?*" she repeated, this time angry.

"Why do you think all your friends hang around with you, Emma? It's not your charming personality. It's because you know all the *boys*, Emma. And all the boys know *you*."

"I am *not* a *slag*!" she shouted back, getting the gist of what Cal was saying.

"Oh, right. Funny, that, 'cause Paulo West said you were a cracking lay. That you'd do anything he wanted. Remember that time you and him stopped the elevator, Emma? And you did it right there?"

The crowd laughed at that one. Paulo West – Emma's ex – had been shooting his mouth off for a while about their adventurous love life. Most people knew about it – including those gathered in the corridor, evidently – but the news had never got to Emma or Rob.

Cal had been informed about it by Joel. Right now it seemed just about the sharpest weapon to strike with, and he used it. Emma had hurt him *so* bad. He wanted to hurt her back.

"You *shit*! We *never*!"

The crowd's laugh redoubled, and it was making Emma mad. She didn't like to be laughed at. She wasn't used to it. It was throwing her off, putting her on the defensive. That was fine with Cal.

"I reckon you *would* have gone with me," Cal continued. "You've held at least three conversations with me by now. By your past record, it's way time we got it together."

"Shut *up!*" she howled, backing away like a cornered animal, flinching away from the grinning faces of the mob that had turned against her.

"Ah, you're not worth it, anyway," Cal said. "You're that second-hand, I don't think I want you."

That really got to her. That was too much. For a second, Cal thought she was going to spring at him, so angry did she look. But then she turned and ran, the laughter of the crowd in her ears, her face burning red. He'd decimated her in front of her audience. She would *never* forgive him for that.

He didn't care. He was done with her. The heat of his rejection spent, he felt small and scared again. Shoving his hands back into his pockets, he sloped away through the dispersing knots of onlookers, thinking of the feel of Emma's breath on his lips and how close they had been.

Cal found he couldn't concentrate on the words that skimmed beneath his eyes. He got about three pages into his new book before realizing that he hadn't a clue what had happened so far. He was mad, or pissed off, or sad or embarrassed or *some* damn thing. He didn't know. It was like all these emotions were shouting so loud in his head that it all blended into a meaningless jumble. He felt depressed and elated at the same time; trapped and freed; angry and sad.

Whatever. He knew one thing, though; the rare inner peace that he'd managed to attain by torching that riverside factory had been shattered already. Didn't they *understand*? Didn't they know what they were doing to him? Joel, Abby, Emma, all of them . . . why couldn't they just leave him to get on with his life? Why did they insist on tormenting him? Yeah, even Joel. No matter how much Cal was angry with him, he couldn't stop worrying about him. He'd dug a hole for himself, and now he was neck-deep in shit. That troubled him.

He put his book back into his bag and ferreted around until he found a sketch pad and a soft pencil. Then he began to draw, savage swoops of lead across the page, pouring out all his emotion into his picture. He sat there for a time, hunched over, his face intense, scrawling a picture, not knowing what it was yet but watching it take shape beneath his pencil.

"Whoa, what is *that*?" said a voice by his shoulder.

He jumped. Abby was sitting on the science steps next to him. He had been so intent on his picture that he hadn't even noticed her approach.

"Don't you know when to give *up*?" he snapped.

"What have *I* done?" Abby asked in disbelief.

"You know what you've done," Cal replied bitterly. "Don't bother trying to fake me out any more. Emma already pulled the punchline on me. So you can drop the act now."

"Oh," Abby said dully. She brushed her hair away from her face with both hands and rested her elbows on her knees, her fingers knitted behind her head.

"Yeah, *oh*," Cal said. After a moment, he sagged. "Look, I'm not going to lay into you or anything like that. I doubt it would make any difference. I'm just asking you, just please leave me alone. For good. Like, don't *speak* to me again or anything."

"Oh God, Cal, I'm sorry," she said. "It's like, this whole stupid joke just got out of hand. I didn't want it to end up like this. I feel like shit about it."

"Good," Cal said. "That brightens my afternoon more than you could know."

"Don't be pissed at me," Abby pleaded.

"Why *not?*" Cal said venomously. "Why the hell not? What did I ever do to you, anyway? I mean, for Emma to do this to me was pathetic enough, but *you?* I never even *met* you. What did I *do?*"

"You were better than me," said Abby, her voice small and ashamed. She crossed her arms in her lap and looked down at the floor. "You beat me in the art competition."

Cal was dumbstruck. Then he began to laugh, short and cruel and acerbic. "Because I beat you in an *art* competition? Oh, you are a *special* kind of shallow."

"I know," she said, unable to meet his gaze. Now that was a turn-up; usually it was Cal who couldn't handle eye contact.

Something in her voice stopped him laughing, though. It sounded genuine. And that was strange. She really did sound like she hated herself for what she'd done.

Are you just kidding yourself again, Cal? You should have learned by now!

"Can I talk to you about something?" she said, raising her head.

"Please, do you think I'm gonna fall for it a second time?" Cal said sarcastically.

"No, I mean it," she said, her wide copper eyes pleading.

"Tell you what," Cal said. "You don't spin me any crap about how you or Emma supposedly fancy me, and you can talk."

"Okay. Deal," Abby said, smiling faintly. "You know, you're a lot more chatty when you're pissed off at me."

Cal shrugged. She was right. When he was angry, he didn't feel shy. When he was aggressive, he stopped mumbling and freezing up. Forget crack, he thought, maybe I should take up PCP.

"Look, Cal, I don't want us to be enemies, okay?" Abby said earnestly.

"Nor do I," he replied quietly.

"I'm *sorry*, okay? What I did . . . it was a mistake. I can't say it enough. I didn't really think about what I was doing. I don't expect you to forgive me, but I'd rather you didn't hate me."

"It wasn't really you, it was more Emma. . ." he said, inwardly wincing as he did so. He was making excuses for her, already willing to forgive her despite what she had done to him. Anyone else, no. But *her* . . . why did she have this *power* over him? "Anyway, why should it bother you?" Cal finished, being deliberately obtuse because he was supposed to be mad at her.

"Because it does," Abby replied, not really giving him an answer.

Cal looked at her oddly. She really did seem sorry.

And against his better judgement, he found himself believing her. His anger was fading fast now, but as yet the shyness hadn't welled up to replace it. He tried to relax a little – *stop jumping on her, she's trying to apologize* – and was surprised to find that he could. It was dangerously easy in his present company.

"I know my track record hasn't been so great," she said. "But I don't want you to be thinking that I'm trying to set you up every time I talk to you. You know, it'd be nice if we could . . . get along, right?"

Cal smiled faintly. "Abby, what are you trying to do? This is just 'cause you feel bad and you want to make yourself feel better."

"I'm trying to make it *up* to you," she protested. "Damn, you can be a defensive son of a bitch sometimes."

"Years of practice," he replied. "I'm just saying, don't make any promises you can't keep."

"I *want* to, though," she said.

"We'll see," Cal replied, his tone neutral.

Abby gave him a fey sort of smile. "Maybe we will."

There was silence between them for a moment. Cal was waiting for the crushing, boiling shyness to kick back in, but for some reason it wasn't happening. Talking to Abby, even in a painfully honest conversation like this one, it seemed . . . *natural?* Yeah, he guessed that was the word. It was almost like with Joel . . . not quite, but almost. And that was a feeling out of all proportion to the time he had known her and the way she had treated him.

"So, you said you wanted to talk to me about some-thing. What's up?"

"Nothing's *up*," she said. "There's something I want to get off my chest, is all."

Cal's expression froze for a second, and then broke into a wicked smile. He coughed into his fist to try and hide it, reluctant to let her see. Unwittingly, she'd tapped right into his gutter sense of humour, and he'd been surprised enough so that he'd forgotten himself for a moment.

"Not *that*," she said, shoving him playfully as she realized what she'd said. "Bad choice of words."

"Works for me," he said, unable to resist the jab now that the tension between them had been broken.

"Shut *up*, I'm trying to tell you something," she said, laughing at her own embarrassment.

Cal turned his attention back to his picture for a moment. Now the lines were more gentle, not so jagged as they had been before.

"So what were you gonna say?" he said, when her laughter had died down a little.

"You know what? It doesn't matter. You've killed the mood now," she joked. A moment later, she got to her feet. "I'm gonna go. I'm really sorry about what me and Emma were doing. I promise – *promise* – I won't do it again."

"Okay," Cal said quietly.

"Maybe we can, y'know, say hi to each other or something sometime," she said.

"Sure," he replied brightly.

"See ya," she said.

"Bye."

And then she walked away, her black hair swinging behind her, and disappeared around the corner.

Cal was thinking about that encounter throughout the rest of the day. Did she mean it? Didn't she? Was she just being friendly, or was she just setting him up for another fall, this time more craftily than Emma?

It didn't matter. He couldn't help the way Abby and Emma made him feel when they talked to him like that. It was the same with any guy, he reasoned. Both of them were pretty, both of them were devastatingly attractive in their own ways; nobody could help feeling just a little warm and toasty inside when they were sitting next to them. The combination of Abby and Emma together was potentially lethal to any red-blooded male.

As for Emma, he couldn't care less now. He knew what she was about. Bitch. He wouldn't be suckered again by her.

But Abby . . . well, with Abby he still wasn't sure. *Was* it all a ruse? She seemed . . . *different* somehow to Emma. There was something about her that wasn't quite right, that didn't quite slot in with the other members of Emma's gang. Was it just because she was the new girl? Or was he just romanticizing wildly?

He had to be careful, that was all. Abby could be setting him up again. If he allowed himself to be fooled *twice*, he'd never survive the hassle he'd get from Joel. He'd climbed a great big mountain of hope and been knocked down once by Emma; but it was like, when

Abby had begun talking to him, he couldn't help picking himself up and climbing again. He was beginning to believe that she was genuine, and he couldn't stop himself.

If he fell another time, he didn't think he could take it.

The bell rang for the end of school, finally bringing an end to the death sentence that was double French. Mrs Hopper, as usual, kept them behind for about five minutes while she finished her lesson. Cal scratched at the table with the end of his pair of compasses. It wasn't the class's fault if their flouncing troll of a French teacher couldn't finish her lessons on time; why did *they* have to suffer? Why couldn't they do it like in those programmes about American schools, where they run off as soon as the bell rings, even if the teacher is in mid-sentence. He bet that in America none of the teachers said primly: "The bell is for *me*, not *you*," before rattling on to finish the exercise they were doing.

Obsessing about the unfairness of the school system in general, he wandered up the drive towards the bus lay-by. He always had to brave the crowds of kids waiting for their buses on the way home; it was a regular part of school life. He had learned by now to become invisible, a pale spectre drifting through the debris of teenagers, passing through unnoticed. Halfway up, he vaguely remembered that this was the way Joel would be going as well; but by then he couldn't be bothered to change course. If he saw Joel, he saw him. He'd just have to deal with it.

Then he was passing through the lay-by, head down. Trying to be invisible.

Today, however, he wasn't invisible enough.

"You! Oi! I want a word with you!"

He didn't know how he knew that those words were addressed to him. He just knew. And he knew by their tone that it wasn't going to be a friendly word at that.

He turned towards the source of the sound in time to see Rob Oakley muscling through the crowd to get to him. He caught just a glimpse of the snarling anger on his face before a fist came out of nowhere and cracked across his jaw. A blast of white annihilated his vision for a second. Cal didn't even really feel the punch; it was the shock and surprise that hit him harder.

Then Rob really piled into him, knocking him to the ground. He pinned one arm under his back and tried to punch at his face, but Cal shoved him off with his free arm. They rolled and fought, Rob trying to get a punch in while Cal was frantically defending against his much larger opponent.

Rob landed a couple of glancing blows, but Cal was as slippery as an eel and Rob couldn't get any weight behind them. They scrambled at each other on the ground and Cal was struck by a thought that seemed ridiculously out of place in their situation: *we must look so stupid doing this.*

Then Rob managed to clout him around the ear, and it stopped being silly and became serious again. He pushed the bigger lad off and got to his feet. A circle had formed around them, chanting "Fight! Fight! Fight!" Strangely predictable, but then this whole encounter also had a kind of surreal aspect to Cal. He felt like he wasn't really in control of himself, that things were just *happening* to him and it was all he could do to stand by and watch while the small and frightened kid that was him got ready to face another of Rob's onslaughts.

It came almost instantly, without either of them pausing for breath. Rob flew in with a flurry of blows to Cal's stomach, and Cal hit back feebly at his ribs, they tangled, half-wrestling and half-boxing. . .

. . .and then rough hands were on them both, dragging them apart. Cal looked over his shoulder to see the massive frame of Mr McLeder, and some tall bearded black guy who he'd never seen before was holding Rob back.

"You son of a bitch!" Rob spat at Cal, writhing helplessly in the black guy's grip. "You're dead for what you done to her! You mess with Emma, you mess with me, you bastard! And if you touch my girlfriend, I'll bloody kill you!"

"You two boys *calm down!*" McLeder bellowed, but Cal ignored him.

"I never!" he cried out. "I never touched her at all."

"I said *stop it!*" McLeder roared, shaking Cal. That shut them both up. "What the *hell* is going on here?"

Both of them were silent.

"*Well?*" he shouted, shaking Cal by the arms again.

"Don't ask me, I know less than you do," he replied sullenly.

"What happened?" McLeder persisted, addressing anyone near by.

It was the black man in the trenchcoat who spoke. "I saw it start. This one attacked that kid there."

Rob's eyes burned. McLeder fixed him with a frosty glare. "True or false, Mr Oakley?"

"True," he muttered in a small voice.

McLeder let go of Cal, who stepped away and began rubbing some circulation back into his arms.

"He was touching up my girlfriend!" Rob blurted suddenly, making another lunge for Cal. He was held fast. "She told me. They were talking, and he got her alone, and he . . . she was in tears when she told me! He should be expelled!"

"What? *What*? That is such *bullshit*!" Cal cried. He half-expected McLeder to roast him then and there for swearing, but McLeder let it slide for once in his life.

"Is this true?" McLeder said from behind him, unmistakable menace in his voice.

"No!" Cal said.

"Liar!" yelled Rob.

"Screw you! Ask anyone! We had an argument in the corridor, and I *beat* her, okay? Everyone saw it. She ran off 'cause she'd lost the argument. And she went and found you, and she got you to do her dirty work for her!"

"Get stuffed, you little freak!" Rob shouted.

"She *used* you, Rob. Ask anyone."

"Alright, that's enough," McLeder said, daring Rob to respond. "Mr Oakley, come with me. As for you, Sampson, you may be assured that I will look into these allegations, and if they are true, your career at Bishop Grove will come to a very sudden end."

He grabbed Rob roughly out of the hands of the black guy and dragged him through the bus crowds

back towards school. The air was buzzing with excitement and chatter. It wasn't often that they got to see
entertainment of this calibre.

"You alright, Sampson?" said the black guy in a deep
bass voice.

"My name's Cal," he replied.

"Cal. Sorry. You need a ride home? You look pretty
sore."

"I'll live," Cal replied sullenly.

"I'm sure you will. Now, do you want a lift home or
not?"

"No thanks," Cal mumbled, looking away. "I'll walk."

The black guy looked at him curiously for a moment.
Cal was still red from the exertion of the fight, but he
seemed to be almost visibly shrinking from the
mouthy, surly lad that he had at first seemed. It was all
in the body language. He was no longer making eye
contact with anyone; his head had dipped a little; his
narrow shoulders were sloped, his voice had got quieter and his sentences shorter. He was shifting around
furtively, wanting to get away from the attention he
had drawn to himself. The other man thought he'd
seen that kind of behaviour before. . .

"I'd really like to talk with you for a moment, Cal,"
the man said, his tone quietly insistent. "You'll be safe
with me. I'm with the police."

Cal felt a tremor in his nerves, sinking into his stomach, which fluttered and jumped. "You got any ID?" he
asked. He might have been frightened, but he wasn't
going to get into a car with a total stranger.

Deerborn produced his identification and gave it to

Cal. A murmur swept around the crowd as a couple of kids read it over his shoulder and relayed the information to their friends.

To Cal, it seemed easier just to give in. He couldn't face the idea of walking through the crowds at the bus lay-by. His cloak of invisibility had been torn away by Rob; now everyone would be looking at him as he passed. Whoever this guy was, he seemed dead set on talking to Cal about something, and it would be better to do it in a car on the way home than out here with all these people about. It was the lesser of two evils. He just wanted to go home.

"Okay," he muttered.

"Come on, then."

They walked in silence back to the car park, where a dark green Peugeot was waiting. The tall guy zapped it with his keys and they got in. He keyed the ignition and started it up. A deafening blast of dance music exploded out of the speakers, making them both jump violently. He swore and stabbed the power button to kill it.

"Sorry," he said, as the engine purred into life. "I always do that. My name's Ben Deerborn."

"Cal," he muttered in reply, even though he'd already told the man his name. *Come on, get driving, I want this over with.*

As if he had heard Cal's thoughts, Deerborn pulled the car out of its bay and headed for the main road. "Where are we going?" he said.

"Ashcroft Road," Cal said quietly.

"Excuse me?"

Cal coughed and repeated himself, louder this time.

"Okay, here we go," he said, turning left on to the road and away from the school.

Cal sat in the passenger seat, looking out of the window. He was concentrating on trying not to be sick. He felt trapped, locked in this car. He should have walked. Why hadn't he *walked*? But that would have looked suspicious, and he had a feeling that Deerborn was suspicious of him already, though he couldn't think why. He seemed to know something . . . there had to be a reason why he was so intent on talking to him. Cal's hands were trembling. Maybe he should ask if he could get out now?

No! Don't be weak! Just hold on for a few minutes, and you'll be home. Hold on.

After a little while, when it became apparent that Cal wasn't going to ask Deerborn why he wanted to talk, Deerborn decided to speak himself.

"I suppose you're wondering why I was at your school," he said. "As I said, I work for the police. I investigate fires, to determine how they were started, and whether they were intentional or not."

Cal swallowed back the vomit that jumped into his throat. His whole body felt shaky now. Him! Deerborn was after *him*! Shit! He could almost feel his guilt showing on his face. Now what the hell was he supposed to do? He was caught, caught, caught, cau—

"I've been going round all the schools in the area, talking to the teachers. Some factory on the riverside got burned down yesterday. A witness said it was a teenager who did it. I don't suppose you know anything about it?"

Cal tried to speak and gagged instead.

"Are you okay? You don't look too well," Deerborn commented. It could have been concern in his voice, or it could have been suspicion.

Cal forced himself to take a breath, to calm himself down. It was like he was crying out his guilt. He had to chill, level out, stop acting so nervous. But he *couldn't*. So there was only one thing to do. He took a few more deep breaths and then spoke, concentrating totally on keeping his voice steady and audible.

"I have this thing," he said. "I freeze up around strangers. I can't talk. To them. Sorry."

Deerborn glanced across at him as he turned right on to another road, this one hedged in by terraced houses. The memories crowded out of the trapdoor in his mind where he kept them locked away during the day. His son, his sweet Carl. He remembered him coming home in tears one day, after a long couple of weeks when he had seemed very quiet and depressed. Eight, he had been, or thereabouts. It was always the quiet kids who got bullied. And Carl had been so sensitive and intro-verted, so terrifyingly fragile.

Deerborn had seen to the bullies, but the damage was done. Carl never quite recovered from the ordeal. He bruised and scarred so easily, not physically but mentally, and he was slow to heal.

Now he remembered why Cal's slump-shouldered, mumbling attitude had seemed familiar. It was the same way his son had been after the incident – a tiny, unobtrusive presence, trying not to be noticed, obsessed with his own thoughts. It had broken his heart to see his son like that, turned into an under-confident bundle of nerves by a thoughtless act of childhood cruelty.

He came back to himself, shaking off the memories, shoving them back into the sealed-off compartment in his mind. As he did so, he realized that they were almost at Ashcroft Road. He had fallen silent, and Cal had been glancing at him uneasily, wondering at the sudden stop in the conversation.

"Sorry," he said. "I was miles away." As he said it, he felt that it sounded a little rude, that a better explanation was needed for apparently ignoring the kid's heartfelt confession. "My son had the same problem," he added. He couldn't go any further, and Cal didn't press him.

"S'okay," he muttered.

"Where's your house?"

"Just here."

Deerborn pulled the car over in front of the large detached house. "Well, good to meet you, Cal. Do me a favour, huh? Keep your ears open for anything about that fire."

"Okay," Cal muttered, getting hurriedly out of the car. "Thanks."

He shouldered his bag and went to his front door, never looking back. Fumbling with the keys, he let himself in, closing the door behind him.

Deerborn's gaze lingered on the front of the house for a time. Teenage kid, wearing outsize clothes, with thatchy brown hair. The descriptions from both the farmer and the tramp were sketchy at best, but this kid fitted them like a glove. He'd seen it the moment he'd spotted him at the lay-by. Could he be the one? It was certainly beginning to look like his earlier guess was wrong; someone was setting fires on purpose. But this kid? It didn't seem to fit.

Doesn't it? Or is it that you don't want it to because he reminds you of Carl?

Deerborn shook his head. He looked once more at the house, his gaze suspicious, and then he drove slowly away.

Chapter Seven

Blaze

"So what's happening, homey?" Joel said as he sat down on the stool next to Cal in chemistry the next day. He was wearing a striped beanie hat and enormously baggy clothes. The bruises on his face had mostly faded to yellowy patches.

Cal didn't answer, ignoring him. The room was filled with the sound of scraping stools, the thump of books on tables and low chatter as the class flooded into the lab. A huge periodic table dominated one wall, next to a tall fume cabinet that looked like an empty bookcase, and the wooden bench-tops were dark with meaningless graffiti.

"Oh come on, don't pretend you're still mad at me. I can tell you're not. When you're pissed off your mouth goes all poochy at the edges."

"Shut up, it does *not*!" Cal replied indignantly.

"Yeah it does," Joel said in his flamboyant (and slightly lisping) voice. "You get this little thing going just at the corner of your mouth, and you stomp around in those great big army boots of yours, and you go all quiet and wounded. I've seen it."

"Yeah? That's good coming from you. When you get mad, your face scrunches up, and you get this expression like a bulldog licking piss off a nettle. Except with stupid hair."

"Sorry, style guru," Joel replied, enjoying himself immensely. "I forgot that the just-out-of-electrotherapy look was in this season."

"You suck."

"Not as much as your momma. Boys down the snooker club call her Vax."

Cal snorted back a laugh. "Yeah well. Your momma's so fat, you can slap her thigh and surf the wave."

"Your momma's so ugly, when God put teeth in her face he ruined a perfectly good butt," Joel went on.

"*Your* momma's got legs like stereos," Cal retorted. "She can't walk—"

"But she *sounds* good," they chorused together.

They were both smiling.

"You've always been crap at holding grudges," Joel said, his narrow face beaming.

"Only 'cause I hate to see a dumb animal suffer."

Joel let that one pass graciously without a comeback. Cal didn't press the advantage. It was Joel's way of saying he was sorry for whatever he had done, even if he didn't really understand what it was. Cal appreciated that. It made him feel better.

"Heard about your fight with Rob. Nice one," Joel said.

"Gave him the old one-two and he dropped like a sack of shit," Cal replied, jabbing the air.

"*Such* a liar," Joel replied. "Way I hear, McLeder and some other guy broke you two up."

"You believe what you wanna believe," Cal said.

Joel laughed, then went a little more serious. "I heard it was about Emma Cobley."

Cal relayed the story of what had happened to him yesterday. The only thing he left out was the incident with Deerborn afterwards. He didn't want Joel to know about the fires. If Joel could keep secrets, then he could too.

"So, what, is Rob after you now?" Joel asked when he had finished.

"I don't know. I reckon by now he'll have found out what really happened. Enough people saw us shouting at each other in the corridor. I think once he knows that Emma lied to him, he's gonna be more concerned with kicking *her* ass than mine."

Their conversation was interrupted by the entrance of McLeder, whose presence dampened the chatter to a barely audible whisper. He dumped his folders on the bench-top in front of the blackboard and began his lesson instantly, as was typical for him.

Once again, Cal's mind wasn't on the lesson. He had never been academically brilliant, and he blamed it on his scatty attention span. His mother – on one of the rare occasions that she actually bothered to talk to him – had informed him that it was because he was part of the soundbite generation, and that children's minds were being wasted away by TV. At least, that was the latest scare in the bog roll she called a newspaper.

He was thinking of three things. The first was Abby. He could see her sitting near the front of the room, on one of the far benches. She was wearing a black pair of dungarees over a blue-and-white striped T-shirt. He watched the way her sheened hair cascaded down her back as she tilted her head upward to read what was being written on the board. Did she mean what she had said, or didn't she? Was she just being friendly? Was it sympathy? Or was it something more? Was she really more than the shallow, unobtainable girl he had always taken her for, or was it all an act to set him up for another cruel trick?

Then there was Joel. He was happy that Joel had been the first to repair the bridge between them, but how long would it last? How long before the inevitable happened, and Joel left him behind? They had been such good friends before, but recently it hadn't been so great. And now one of Joel's new friends had got him into trouble, and Cal had been dragged into it. That was a hassle that he didn't need right now, on top of Abby and Emma being such a pair of bitches, but it was hardly something he could ignore.

Third and last, there was Deerborn. Shit, until yesterday he'd never thought for one minute that setting those fires would ever get him caught. He hadn't been thinking about anything except the peace that he found at the heart of the blaze. But now there was this guy, this policeman, and he didn't know why but he could *tell* that Deerborn knew something when he was talking to him in the car. Even before he'd got him in the car, he knew something. Cal didn't like it.

Then stop setting the fires, he thought to himself. But he knew that he couldn't do that. Not now, not with everything going on. It was like the world was conspiring to mess with his head, and the only thing that could stop him from going insane from the pressure was the fire...

If everyone would just leave him alone, if everything would just go back to how it was before his life became complicated, then it would all be okay. But until then, he had to ride the storm and cope with it in any way he could.

After a lengthy explanation of the experiment that they were going to do – which Cal had completely missed – they were told to collect the chemicals they needed and to begin. Joel, who had been noting them down, told him to go and get the iodine while he picked up the rest of the stuff. He shuffled away, waiting meekly by the crowded iodine rack until everybody had got one of the heavy bottles. Then he took one himself and ambled back towards his bench. McLeder was talking to some girl at the front of the class.

He caught sight of Abby on the other side of the room, returning from the stack of petri dishes with a few in her hand. She met his gaze. He dropped it automatically... then dared to look up again. She smiled at him and waved hello. He smiled back nervously and looked away.

His body was flushed with exhilaration; his skin tingled, his eyes were not seeing what was in front of him.

And he walked into the edge of a table, knocking his hip hard against it, aggravating the bruises that he still had from last night's beating. The next thing he heard was a loud, heavy smash, and he realized that the bottle of iodine wasn't in his hand any more. It was in a pool by his feet, spattered in a huge starburst across the floor. It was all over his scruffy trainers. But that wasn't important. What was important was that the whole class was looking at him.

And then they began jeering, clapping and whooping.

He knew that it happened to anyone who dropped anything in a science lab. But with him, it seemed like each person was really *laughing* at him, at how small and pathetic and spineless he was. He felt the warm flush of excitement turn sour, turning into embarrassment, and he wanted to get out of there. But once more, there was nowhere to go.

"Sampson!" McLeder cried. For a moment, Cal thought that the teacher was going to roast him then and there, in front of everybody, but then McLeder's face softened a little. "Go to the caretaker's office," he said. "Get something to clear that up."

It was a glorious reprieve. Head down, he scurried out of the room and away from the amused gazes of his classmates. And of Abby.

Joel watched him go, sighing to himself. There went one seriously messed-up kid. He glanced over at Abby. He'd seen her smile at him. That had probably been why Cal had dropped the iodine, he reckoned. Then she had laughed along with the rest of them.

He was going to do something about her, he promised himself.

His chance came much sooner than he thought. McLeder had barely resumed the lesson before the secretary, Mrs Flack, gave a cursory knock and then strode across the lab, propelling herself with enviable speed and dexterity on her high heels. She walked over to McLeder and began talking to him quietly. All work surreptitiously stopped while everyone tried to hear what the message was about. McLeder's brow furrowed, and then he said something to the secretary and she left.

A moment later, he turned back to the class. "I'm leaving for a few minutes. I trust that you'll be quiet and keep working while I'm gone."

Not expecting a response – and knowing that it would be a lie anyhow – he left the class alone.

There was a gap of about five seconds to allow McLeder to get to minimum safe distance before the pupils erupted into a babble. What had Flack been to see him about? It must have been important, or why would McLeder have looked so concerned?

But those questions didn't interest Joel. Instead, he got up from his chair and slipped across the room to where Abby Cohen was sitting. She looked up as he plonked himself on the edge of her bench-top. For a moment, her smooth face crinkled in puzzlement, then she returned to the usual expression that she wore when Joel talked to her. It was a sort of slightly condescending, distasteful set to her features, saying: *what am I doing talking to you?*

"So," he said, shuffling on the bench until he was comfy.

"So what?" Abby replied.

"What's going on with you and Cal, then?" Joel said, scratching under the collar of his beanie.

"Like I should tell you," Abby replied. "Since when did we become best friends?"

"Cut the crap," Joel said. "I don't want to be friends with you. What I do want is for you to stop screwing around with Cal."

"Sod off, Joel," Abby snapped. "It's nothing to do with you."

"Yeah, it is. He's my friend. And he's messed up enough as it is without you and Emma sticking your oars in."

"It's touching that you're willing to stick up for him," Abby said sarcastically. "You know, I don't often see you two hanging around together at lunchtimes. Weird, that, when you two are such good friends."

"I'm not the one that's playing around with him," Joel replied venomously.

"Yes, you are," she said. "You just aren't being honest about it. What is it, you're best buddies out of school but he's not cool enough to have around when you're with the guys down the track?"

"You just have no idea what you're talking about, do you?"

"I've got a better idea than *you* have. Look, I'll tell you what's going on, not that you'll believe me. I *was* messing around with Cal. Now I'm not. Okay?"

Joel leaned closer. He looked angry, but Abby didn't

flinch. "Alright, I'll tell *you* what's going on. You might have noticed while you were playing your little game that Cal is a nervous breakdown waiting to happen; and you and Emma have done nothing but make it worse since you started getting in his face. You just don't know what you're *doing*, okay? You haven't seen what he's become like."

"What's he become like?" Abby interjected suddenly. She sounded almost concerned, Joel thought with surprise.

"Don't worry yourself about it. Just stop whatever you're doing, okay? Don't wind him up, don't mess with him, just . . . just leave him alone. It's not funny any more, alright? Just stop it."

He slid off the edge of the table and walked away from her, back to his spot on the other side of the room. Abby looked back at the scrawls on her textbook, not really seeing them, thinking about what he had said.

Cal's footsteps steadily slowed as he walked along the empty, hollow corridors, following the tempo of his decelerating heart. He leaned against a wall and allowed himself to relax a little. Today, he couldn't be bothered getting angry at himself for being so clumsy; he had too many other things on his mind to care.

But one thing did get him, like a spike in his breastbone. He had seen Abby after he had dropped the beaker. She had been laughing. Like everyone else. Only Joel hadn't been laughing, because he knew what Cal was like. But Abby? Was she just following the crowd, or did she really mean it? He knew he was being oversensitive, but he really couldn't stop himself.

Tapping the heel of his army boots against the wall behind him, he stayed there for a while until he was calm again. After that, he headed for the caretaker's office.

The caretaker was known simply as The Caretaker. If he'd had a name to attach to the face – balding, gaunt and bespectacled – then Cal might have felt worse about flicking all those fag-butts into his back garden on the way to school every morning. But as it was, he was just this . . . *cleaning* guy, this creature that had no purpose in life other than to sweep the school corridors like a sentinel, eliminating rubbish and mopping up spills wherever they reared their evil heads. Allegedly, he was married; but nobody had ever seen whoever he was supposed to be married *to*. Cal entertained himself with notions of an obese, whiskered ogress who never left the house but feasted on the bones of children from the nearby primary when they strayed too close.

He arrived at the office. It was a blank wooden door, like a storage cupboard, with "CARETAKER" stencilled on it and a Yale lock. He knocked.

The door opened after a moment, and The Caretaker peered out of a haze of cigarette smoke. It was always smoky in there – The Caretaker and the dinner ladies all fagged it something special, and it was a tiny room with hardly any ventilation.

"I spilt some iodine in one of the labs," Cal said. His voice was clear and easy, like it was with Joel. Even Cal couldn't bring himself to be intimidated by The Caretaker.

"Right, okay, I'll get the mop," he said in a gloomy monotone. He disappeared back inside for a minute. Cal watched him through the fog, searching around the room. After a few moments, he emerged again. "I know where it is. I left it in A104. I'll go and get it for you."

"Thanks," Cal said, as The Caretaker swept past him in his stiff, robotic walk, pulling the door closed behind him.

Cal waited in the corridor, looking down at the iodine-spattered toes of his shoes. It was already staining the black leather a sort of browny colour. He didn't really care; they were half knackered anyway.

A moment later, he heard a soft sliding, and looked to where it had come from. The Caretaker's office door was ajar. A thin line of dimness beckoned invitingly between the door and the jamb. He mustn't have closed it hard enough for the latch to click.

And then suddenly there was something forming in Cal's mind. Something dark and massive. An idea. No: a *solution.* A way to finish everything.

Cal, you can't be thinking *this.*

But he was. He couldn't stop himself. In one moment, he had been struck and possessed by the simplicity of what had to be done. And the idea was so *glorious.*

Glancing up and down the empty corridor, he pushed open the door to The Caretaker's office and slipped inside.

It was drab and gloomy within, the chilly autumn sunlight from outside muted by the cigarette smoke. A couple of cupboards leaned against the walls, and a desk was placed under the meagre slatted windows. Chairs were placed about, making the small room crowded. Usually they were taken up by the dinner ladies, but it was late in the day now and they had all gone home.

He shut the door behind him, clicking the latch home. The door could be opened from the inside without a key. Quickly, he glanced around. He was aware that he didn't have a lot of time. A104 was not far away. The Caretaker would be back any second. Coughing as the acrid smoke teased his lungs, he looked around.

The desk.

He hastened over to it and began pulling out drawers. The first one was full of magazines. He rummaged down through them, half-expecting to find a pile of pornos. He was disappointed. They were all boring special-interest magazines or tabloid glossies.

Closing that one, he went for the drawer below. His breathing was shallow now, his hands clammy. If he was caught in here, the teachers would eat him alive. He wasn't afraid of The Caretaker, but of who The Caretaker would report him to. And knowing his luck, it'd be McLeder.

The next drawer was taken up by a few loose pencils and a couple of thin, hardback notebooks. Account ledgers, for keeping track of the money spent on cleaning equipment. Other assorted junk was scattered around the interior; he sifted through it rapidly and found nothing.

Come on, come on!

Slamming the drawer closed a little too loudly in his haste, he moved on down to the bottom one. He was just sliding it open when he heard the creak of swing doors and the sounds of footsteps in the corridor outside, a heavy tap that was getting louder.

Ignore it, he thought. *Bound to be people passing by outside.*

He looked down into the drawer. A Tupperware box full of paperclips, a ball of string, some—

Someone hammered at the door. He started violently, banging his elbow against a nearby chair with a loud scraping sound.

Shit!

He went quiet. They *must* have heard that. For a moment, there was a terrible silence, as he waited, not daring to move, his breathing almost silent. *Go on, piss off, there's nobody here!*

The hammering came again. Whoever that person was, they knew how to knock alright.

Cal closed his eyes, mentally willing whoever was outside to leave. There was silence again from the person in the corridor, the kind of *waiting* silence given off by people when their patience is going to run out soon. Cal bit his lip. His eyes were beginning to water because of the smoky atmosphere.

Then there was the squeak of rubber as they turned on the ball of their foot and walked away, their footstep taps diminishing rapidly.

Cal returned to his search, faster and more careless now. He'd lost a lot of time. He rummaged through the bric-à-brac in the bottom drawer, barely noticing what he was shoving aside with his hands, and then his palm closed on what he was searching for. He moaned in relief.

Quickly, he tugged the fat ring of keys out of the drawer. They couldn't be The Caretaker's set, because he always carried them with him, hanging from his belt; Cal figured it was the spares. But damn it, there were so many of them! Cal flicked them by under his fingers, and his despair turned to relief as he saw that they had all been tagged with little sticky labels, and their function written on in pen. He searched through, jingling frantically, and located the ones he needed, then he slid them off the ring, one by one, and dropped them in the pockets of his outsize jeans.

For a moment, the ghost of caution tapped him on the shoulder; what if the missing keys were noticed before he had time to put his plan into effect? But no, that was pretty unlikely. The Caretaker would never notice the theft unless he had cause to use the spare set. And Cal reckoned he'd only need to use the spares if he lost the ones he carried. And that was hardly going to happen over the next few days.

He was about to replace the bundle of keys when he saw what else was in the drawer. A small, laminated booklet. Examining the cover, he saw that it was the operating manual for the burglar alarm system.

I didn't think of that, he thought to himself. But The Caretaker had to have the code to the alarm; and it was too important to trust to one man's memory. It would be written down somewhere. At least, he hoped it was. Otherwise his plan would have foundered before it had even begun. He flicked through the manual, but that revealed nothing.

Where was the code? There had *to be a code!*

He threw the keys back in the drawer and closed it, then scanned the smoke-filled room again. He hadn't seen it in the drawers; he was sure of that. So where would it be? Not in the cupboards, surely? He looked over the desk again, but there was nothing that he hadn't checked. So *where*?

Outside in the corridor, there were more footsteps. Lighter this time. Could it be him? Cal swallowed against the dryness in his throat, trying to think of an excuse why he'd be inside. None sprang to mind.

And then his roving eyes fell on the coat that was hung over the back of one of the chairs. Of course! He set the alarm as the first thing he did when he came in and the last thing before he left; both times he'd be wearing his coat! Instantly, he sprang over to it, plunging his hands into the pockets. Breath mints, cheque book, cotton buds, a pair of dice . . . how much crap did this guy carry around, anyway? The outside pockets didn't yield anything useful, so he tried the inner ones.

The footsteps halted outside the door.

His fingers writhed in the pocket, touching something paper, scrambling to get a hold on it. Could that be it?

A key rattled in the lock.

It's him! It's him!

And then he snagged it, darting across the room and pulling the slip of paper with him where he had scissored it between his fingers. Not knowing what else to do, not even thinking, he pressed himself up against the wall next to the door.

You idiot! This never works except in the movies! He'll see you as soon as he comes in!

But Cal had made his choice now. He held his breath and was still.

The door swung open towards him. He could see The Caretaker in the tiny crack between the hinges. He leaned in, looked around, the mop in his hand . . . and then harumphed and was gone, closing the door behind him with a click.

Cal breathed out slowly. Lucky, lucky, lucky. He looked down at the slip of paper in his hand. Four numbers were written on it in faded pen.

Got it, he thought.

Not wanting to stay here one second longer than he had to, he went to the desk and grabbed a pen and a bit of paper. Taking the slip that he had stolen from The Caretaker's coat, he copied down the numbers that were written on it. Then he replaced the original in the coat pocket, stashed the copy in his jeans, went to the door and listened.

Nobody outside.

He twisted the latch and pulled the door open a crack. From where he could see, there was nobody coming up the corridor. He swung it open and stepped out.

"Sampson!"

Bastard!

McLeder. He had just turned the corner from the science block, stepping into view just as Cal had come out of the office. He was in it deep now. *So* very deep.

He closed the door behind him absently, as if by doing that he could erase the memory of his being there. But McLeder had seen him, no question.

McLeder strode up to him; but there was something odd in his manner. He didn't look angry, just . . . sort of *confused* or something. Cal met him halfway. By that time his throat had already thickened enough to prevent him talking very well, and his head was pounding like a bitch. He looked down at his shoes. He didn't need this.

"Cal," McLeder said, and that was when he knew something was wrong. McLeder *never* called pupils by their first names.

Cal tried to meet his gaze and couldn't.

"Cal, the police are here. They want to talk to you."

Chapter Eight

Dousing

They walked him through the wide, cool reception of the police station. Chequered tiles ran by beneath his downturned gaze. Plastic green chairs were lined up on one side, a waiting area, where eyes turned blank by boredom or bright with worry followed his progress incuriously. He fought for each breath, struggling to pull the stale air into his fluttering lungs, forcing it past his resisting throat. His face burned; his body prickled and itched; his eyes watered.

It was a nightmare, and one that wasn't going to end.

Through the grey corridors of the station he was led, past blank doors and opaque plastic windows. It was grim and drab and unwelcoming; but he had hardly expected anything else. He kept his head down and concentrated on the chequered tiles again, watching them slide under his boots. White, black, white, black . . . it went on and on. Anything to stop him thinking about what was happening.

"Wait in here, please," the officer said, swinging a door open. Inside was a windowless room with a single table and a few chairs. A light burned overhead, throwing harsh, flat illumination. Cal obediently entered and sat down. The door closed behind him, leaving him alone.

He shut his eyes and bit his lip hard enough to hurt.

This'll be alright. It will. They don't know anything. You'll be okay.

But what if he *wasn't* okay? What if he was going to jail? Or one of those juvenile offenders' things?

Screw that. That *wasn't fair!* The fires weren't his fault! He couldn't help it. He wasn't hurting anyone! He was saving *himself.*

Listen to yourself, Cal. You're dangerous. You're right: you can't help setting those fires. And you're gonna do it again. There's a word for people like you. Pyromaniacs. Tell them now and stop yourself. You need help.

No. No way. He couldn't do that. He wasn't admitting to anything. He didn't have enough faith in the police or the courts. He'd sort it out himself, in his own way. He already had his plan, forming and thickening in his mind. All he needed was to get through this.

At least McLeder had been too distracted by the news that the police wanted to see Cal to notice that he had been inside The Caretaker's office. Small mercies, and all that.

The door opened and Ben Deerborn stepped through, carrying with him a portable tape recorder.

He closed the door behind him, laid the recorder on the table and pressed *record* as he sat down.

"Interview with Calhoun Sampson commences 4:07," he began, then went through some other preliminaries such as who was present in the room and the case file number that the recording was relevant to.

When it was all done, Deerborn looked up at Cal. "So, how you doing, Cal?"

"What's. . ." Cal began, realized he wasn't making any sound and began again. "What's all this?" He motioned to the tape recorder.

Deerborn tried to look apologetic, though with his tired eyes and haggard face it only made him look weary. "It's standard policy. We have to record all our interviews."

"Oh," Cal said, then managed: "Have I been arrested?"

Ben looked oddly at the kid squirming in the seat in front of him, apparently desperate to leave. "No. You're here to help with our inquiries. You can leave whenever you want."

Cal hesitated for a moment, then got up and walked to the door.

"But if you do," Deerborn said. "I'll be forced to arrest you on suspicion of arson."

Cal stopped. A tight knot had formed in his stomach and was squeezing itself hard. Reluctantly, he turned and sat down.

"I know you don't like being under pressure," Deerborn said in his mellifluous voice. "I've talked to some of your teachers. But the sooner you co-operate, the sooner we can get this over with."

"Okay," Cal mumbled, looking shiftily towards the door again.

"Alright," Deerborn said, adopting a more businesslike tone. "I won't waste time on pleasantries, because I know you're anxious to get out of here. Can you tell me where you were last Friday night?"

"Poppy's. With Joel."

"This would be Joel Manning?"

Cal nodded.

"Interviewee has nodded yes," Deerborn said into the tape recorder. "And what happened after you left Poppy's?"

"We went home."

"How? Taxi?"

"No, we walked."

"Can you speak up for the tape?"

"We *walked*," Cal said irritably.

"Alright. What route did you take home?"

Cal knew where this was leading, so he lied. "Followed the road. Turned off at Benchley House."

"That's a long way to go."

"I was upset. I needed a walk."

"Really? Why were you upset?"

And so Cal told him about what had happened at Poppy's that night. He had to force the words out, clogged as they were with humiliation and embarrassment.

"Why did you take the road? Isn't there a much more direct route over the fields?"

"Is there?" Cal replied quietly. "I didn't know."

Deerborn tapped his fingers on the table. "Do you know the old riverside factory opposite the textile mill?"

Cal paused convincingly. "Yeah."

"Did you know it was burned down the day before yesterday? A homeless guy was inside at the time."

Cal forced down the shock and horror before it could appear on his face and well up in his stomach. It was a terrible effort, but he kept his face blank. Deerborn was studying him for a reaction.

"Anyway, the guy got out alright," Deerborn went on, still watching Cal for signs of relief. Again, he was just able to keep himself steady. "But he did manage to give us a description of somebody he saw at the site just after the fire. Shortish, thatchy hair, wearing a big black jumper. You got to admit, it's pretty close to you."

Cal opened his mouth to say something, but Deerborn cut him off. "And a hundred other kids, I know. Thing is, when that barn burned down on Friday, I thought it was an accident, but—"

"Hang on, what barn?" Cal jumped in. Deerborn was trying to trick him. He hadn't mentioned the barn before; he wanted Cal to give himself away by letting slip that he knew about it in some way. He wasn't falling for that.

This is too much; I gotta get this over with soon.

Deerborn cleared his throat. He was put out that his ruse hadn't worked. "There was a barn that burned down on Friday, in the fields between Poppy's and your house. Anyway, as I was saying, I thought that was probably accidental. But after this factory fire, well . . . that's a different story. I know that one was on purpose. I found traces of gas containers in the wreckage. So we're looking at arson here. And the same description of this kid was given at both fire spots."

"Do you think I did it?" Cal asked, his voice a hoarse whisper.

"Did you?"

"No."

And so it went on. Deerborn went through the events surrounding the fires over and over again, and Cal's story was always the same. He had no alibi for the factory fire, he said; he was watching TV at home. But that hardly made him guilty. After all, he spent most of his life alone at home. In the end, it became apparent that Deerborn really didn't have anything to go on. Even to Cal's nervous mind, that was obvious. He was a suspect, but that was all.

Eventually, Deerborn grew tired. Cal wasn't going to be caught out by him. That meant he was either cleverer than he looked (and his grades suggested) or he was innocent. He gazed levelly at Cal for a few seconds – which was ineffective since Cal wouldn't meet his eyes – and then leaned over to the tape recorder and said: "Interview terminated, 4:58."

Cal looked up hopefully as Deerborn pushed back his chair, stood up and hit the *stop* button. "Do you want to give your parents a call?"

"They're in London," he said.

"Anyone else who can give you a lift?"

"No."

Deerborn sighed again. He always seemed so weary, Cal thought. Like a huge weight had settled on his shoulders and was gradually crushing him.

"I'll take you, then."

"I'd rather walk," Cal said.

Deerborn looked up. "It's a long way."

"I know."

He shrugged. "Okay."

With that, Cal was gone, without waiting for anyone to show him out.

Deerborn sat back down in his chair. What was the thing that he had about this kid? He was a probable arsonist, and even though the evidence was only circumstantial, it was enough to make him prime suspect. But even so, Deerborn found that he couldn't help going easy on Cal. He could haul him in for an identity parade; he could have Cal's blood tested for cannabis so he had a possible connection to the scrap of a joint he'd found near the farmer's barn. He was a good investigator. He could nail this kid if he tried hard enough.

But he wasn't trying hard enough. Something was holding him back. Was it the kid's shyness? Or was it because he just had this feeling that there were pieces of this puzzle that he didn't understand, and that it would be wrong to go for an easy arrest right now?

But there was another reason. It was because, more and more, he was seeing aspects of Carl in the kid. The way his eyes flickered around, never settling on anything; the way he fidgeted with his fingers. Now he thought about it, even their names were similar. Carl –

Cal. It wasn't as if they *looked* the same – their skin was a different colour, for starters – but they shared so many mannerisms, so many tiny little habits and actions, that he couldn't help thinking of his poor dead son whenever he looked at the kid.

"Oh, this is bull," he said aloud. Then, more quietly, he added: "You're just seeing Carl in your head. You're projecting him on to this kid. It's guilt talking, that's what it is."

Was that it? Was he really just trying to assuage his guilt by going easy on Cal, as if he was some kind of substitute for Carl? Or was he just allowing his personal feelings to get in the way of his professional conduct?

He didn't know. He really didn't know.

It was getting dark by the time Cal came out of the park on to Ashcroft Road. They had closed up the gates with the coming of dusk, but he barely broke stride as he slipped up the gatepost and over the spiked railings. A cold breeze weaved through his tangled hair, stirring the trail of smoke that drifted gently skyward from the glowing tip of his cigarette.

Ashcroft Road was painted in shades of blue and grey, except where the streetlamps cut vicious holes of artificial yellow in the colours of the coming night. Cal dragged savagely on his cigarette and threw the butt over his shoulder, into the park.

He was trembling. He couldn't hold himself still. It had all built up inside him, the stress and humiliation, the self-hate and helplessness, until he felt that his body couldn't contain it any more. Joel, Emma and Abby, and now Deerborn; it was like they were all conspiring to drive him insane, to push his already unbalanced frame of mind right off its moorings.

He had to burn something. He had to. It was the only way.

Plans and possibilities were already pushing themselves to the forefront of his mind, jostling for position as he walked along the road towards his house. The junkyard? No, too big, and guarded. How about somewhere in the Zone, the cluster of derelict buildings over the other side of town? No, it was full of stoners and freaks; he might hurt someone, or get hurt himself. The tip? He could torch one of those huge rubbish skips. Now *that* might work. . .

He reached his house, and was just walking up the drive to the front door when he saw the gate to the back garden swing inward. He stopped where he was, expecting to see Joel; but to his surprise, it was not Joel but Abby that emerged.

"Oh, there you are," she said as she saw him.

Not now. He didn't want to deal with her now. Not on top of everything else. He had to get rid of her, get his stuff from inside, and go torch something. But he couldn't just tell her to go away, could he? And damn it, she was so pretty, standing there.

Screw it. The fire was more important. He couldn't handle her at the moment.

"Cal?" she prompted, when he didn't respond but kept his head down. He walked to his front door and put the key in the lock.

"I can't . . . *talk* to you right now," he said, forcing the words out.

"What happened to you?" she said, drawing closer to him, concern on her face. "I heard you'd been arrested, Amy Keller saw you being taken off by a couple of cops. What happened?"

"Listen, I can't . . . I don't want you around now," he said, leaning his forehead against the door, his hand still holding the key in the lock.

"Cal, you're scaring me. Are you okay?"

He laughed, a short, bitter sound. "I'm scaring you, am I?" His voice dropped to a whisper. "Then what the hell do you think *I* feel like?"

"What's wrong? Cal, what's wrong?"

His voice was barely audible. "I don't want to be like this any more," he said.

And then he started to cry. He couldn't help it. It was as if admitting the fact had unlocked the floodgates inside. He felt it swell up inside him almost physically, and suddenly he couldn't hold it back any more. Still leaning his head against his front door, he cried for all the fear, all the pain and all the turmoil that rested on his back.

He felt an arm laid around him, and he turned into Abby's embrace, and sobbed into her shoulder while she held him. He could feel the warmth of her body, the press of her breasts against his chest; he could smell her hair. They held each other, and he wished it would never end.

But it was a trap, and he knew it, and he pushed her gently away. He needed the fire. The fire, at least, would not betray him.

"Get away from me," he said, more harshly than he had intended. He turned away from the shock and hurt on Abby's face and twisted the key in the lock.

"Why?" Abby cried unexpectedly. "Do you still think I'm playing with you? I'm not, Cal. All that finished a long time ago."

"Whatever. I don't care. Just leave me alone," Cal said flatly, opening the door and stepping inside.

"No. *Hell*, no," Abby said, stepping inside with him, blocking the doorway so that he couldn't shut the door.

"Get out of my house," Cal said wearily.

"Make me," she challenged.

Cal stood there for a minute, his hand on the door as if to shut it. Then he shrugged, let go of it and walked away into the house without a word.

Abby found him in the lounge, sitting cross-legged on the floor, sparking up a fat, loose joint with his smiley-sun Clipper. She sat down opposite him, also cross-legged.

"You close the front door?" he asked, the joint wiggling in his mouth as he spoke.

"Uh-huh," Abby replied.

Cal took a toke, wincing as the hot smoke seared into his lungs. He drew the joint away from his lips and blew out a thick cloud.

"Never was any good at rolling," he said, looking at the construction between his fingers. "Always too harsh. Now Joel, he can roll with the best of 'em." He looked up at her. "Want some?"

"Sure," she said.

"How about a beer?"

"Okay."

Cal got up and went to the fridge, returning with a couple of cold Heinekens and an ashtray. He put one of the beers down in front of her and sat down again. She was still coughing from the toke she had just taken.

"Sweet *shit*, you're right. You really can't roll."

He shrugged. "Told you."

She handed him back the joint, popped her beer and drank some, looking around his lounge as she did so. It had a warm, beige and brown colour scheme to it, with a fireplace against one wall. She looked back at Cal. His face was still red, his cheeks blotchy and his eyes wet from crying, but he seemed to have forgotten all about his earlier breakdown. It was bizarre; one minute he couldn't seem to stand the sight of her, but when she'd pressured him he'd crumbled, and now he was treating her like a guest. This whole thing was way weird.

"I went round the back to see if you were in," she said.

Cal looked at her quizzically.

"You know, that's why I was coming out of your garden when you came home. Sometimes people don't hear the doorbell. I wasn't burgling the place or anything."

Cal shrugged and tapped the ash. "Burgle what you like. None of this stuff is mine. Long as you don't touch my room."

"What, you mean I could just take that TV right now?" Abby said, joking.

Cal's reply was serious, however. "I mean it. I don't care. This stuff isn't *mine*; I've got no attachment to it.

All this stuff belongs to my parents. This place is like . . . their weekend residence. It's the only chance during the week they get to see each other. They work on different sides of London. If something got taken, they'd just replace it. Gotta keep the old homestead fully furnished."

Abby was puzzled by the falsely casual tone in his voice. "So what about you?"

He toked and blew out again. "I'm the career impediment my mum never forgave me for."

"What?"

Cal looked down at the floor between his crossed legs. "I don't care if you know. It doesn't matter what I tell you. In a few days, none of you are gonna be able to hurt me any more."

"What does—" Abby began, but he overrode her.

"So, like, my mum gets pregnant. By accident. And here I am." He swigged his beer. "I probably would have been aborted if not for my grandma. Very religious. She wouldn't let Mum do it. But my parents are *career* people, you see. Doesn't do a career much good if they have to take a year or two out to care for a baby. So they sort of dumped me on Joel's parents, who are nice if a bit ditzy. And then they forgot about me. They give me a little pocket money, enough to keep me going; they pay for what needs paying for, and we leave each other alone. That's the way it is."

Abby felt strange. For some reason, it disturbed her that Cal – who didn't know her very well and certainly didn't *trust* her – was pouring all this out, laying bare all his vulnerabilities for her to see. There was something wrong about it. She felt like she was being given something that she didn't deserve to have.

"What are you telling me this for?" she asked.

"Isn't it what you wanted?" he asked conversationally. He handed her back the joint, which was packed so loose that it had already burned halfway down. "I thought that was why you came in. Come to check out the weird kid, find out what makes him tick. Hell, if you're gonna rip me apart anyway, I might as well give you a few footholds and you can get it over with."

"You still think that, don't you? You still think I'm playing Emma's game."

"Can't think of any other reason why you'd be here."

"That's because you never cut yourself any slack," Abby replied, annoyed. "I'm here because I was worried. I heard about the police, and I was worried. I wanted to see how you were. And you're obviously *not* okay, so that's why I'm here."

"Touched," Cal said sarcastically.

Abby sighed. "Okay, here it is. You probably won't believe me, but I'm gonna tell you anyway. I don't *like* Emma, alright? I don't think anyone really likes Emma. But she's popular, alright? She's like, *the* girl, you know? I'm the new kid. All my friends are over at St Paul's." She paused for a moment. "You remember what I was gonna tell you before, over at the science steps? That was it. I don't like Emma, and I don't like her gang, and you're the only person I can tell because you're the only person I can trust not to tell her."

Cal swigged his beer and looked at her, long and hard. He wasn't shy at the moment, he was too pissed off at everything to be shy. "So why not dump them?"

"It's not that easy," Abby said, brushing her hair back behind her ear. She paused to take a gentle drag on the joint. "Here, you want this? I'm done. It's too hot for me." Cal reached out and accepted it. Abby went on. "Yeah, like I was saying, it's not that easy. If I get on the wrong side of Emma, the whole school is gonna follow her lead. I'm not strong enough to do that. I *want* to be, but I can't. I don't have the guts to go it alone."

There was silence between them for a moment. Cal was digesting what she had said. Did she mean it? He wished he could just *trust* her.

"Do you think I'm shallow?" she said suddenly, her copper eyes meeting his.

"I don't know you well enough to say."

"No, but from what you *do* know. I want you to tell me."

Cal considered for a moment. "At first I thought you were just like the rest of Emma's gang. Now I'm not so sure. But are you gonna mess me around like Emma did, or are you genuine? A lot depends on what you're intending to do with me."

"*Do* with you?" Abby laughed. "What, like you've got no choice in the matter?"

"Not with you, no," he said.

Abby brushed her hair back again unnecessarily. Cal was surprised to hear nervousness in her voice. "You mean that?"

"Yeah. I do," Cal replied. There was no point in anything other than honesty any more.

She shuffled closer to him, uncrossing her legs and

kneeling. Softly, she cupped his face in his hands and leaned towards him. At the last moment, Cal flinched away.

"Don't worry," she said softly. "I know what Emma did to you. There's no one here to see."

And Cal gave in to her. Their lips met and parted, her tongue sliding over his, tasting each other. It was a moment that Cal had fretted about since he was old enough to care; his first real kiss. But to his surprise, it was the easiest and most natural thing in the world. And was it ever glorious. The smell of her, the feel of her touch on his skin, the rhythm of their lips parting and coming together . . . it was so simple, so instinctive, that he couldn't believe he had ever thought it would be anything else.

And it felt good. So good.

After a time, she broke away from him. Their faces still only inches apart, her hands still encircling his jaw, she said softly: "You okay?"

"Uh-huh," he replied, breaking into a smile.

"Thought so," she said, and then she moved into him, and they lay out on the carpet, kissing each other, stroking hair and arms and throat. The joint smouldered, forgotten, in the ashtray. Their beers stood abandoned near by. And for a time, everything faded away but them.

But then Cal pushed her gently away, and looked down at his knees. He resumed his cross-legged position. "Why do you keep on trying to talk to me, if you're not still on this Emma trip?"

"You know what your problem is?" Abby said,

exasperated. "You don't believe in yourself. Not the tiniest bit." She reached for the words to say what she meant. "I'm *trying* to . . . I dunno, get to know you or something, and you think I'm just setting you up for a fall. It makes it really hard, y'know?"

"Yeah, but *why*?"

"You can guess why," she said. "And you're not gonna make me say it."

Cal couldn't stop a little smile from breaking out on his face.

"The thing is," she said, "all the guys Emma keeps trying to throw at me just want to get laid and be done with it. They come on too strong, and they won't take no for an answer. I'm not into that." She leaned forward then. "I think I can trust you, though. To stop when I want you to."

Cal looked a little bewildered. "Sure you can."

"That's cool," she replied, edging closer to him and softly putting her lips on his. He responded, and their arms encircled each other, and they slid to the floor of the lounge, where this time they stayed.

And for Cal, the need to burn faded until it was just an unpleasant memory.

Chapter Nine

Embers

It was Friday. The weather had brightened up a little since the start of the week. The miserable clouds had finally dispersed, and the sun had come out, drying off the lurking puddles and lifting spirits all around. Certainly, it made Bishop Grove look almost cheery to Abby as she walked down the drive to school. She was feeling a lot better about herself, anyway. Today was filled with purpose. Today there was something she had to do.

She was conscious of the curious looks she drew as she joined the crowd spilling down towards the school doors. Someone stifled a laugh; a couple of others seemed impressed. One lad that she didn't know made some complimentary comment as he walked past, and she smiled radiantly at him. She liked the attention. It was past time she'd done something like this. She would have done it long ago, if she thought she could have.

On a whim, she headed around the side of the school, past the bike sheds where Emma and the gang usually hung out before the registration bell called them to class. When she turned the corner, however, there was only Emma there, sitting on the wall and swinging her heels, looking absently out across the playing fields. She looked as if she was waiting for someone. Abby wandered over to her.

"Hey," she said.

Emma turned round and looked at her. For a moment, surprise registered on her features; then she exclaimed: "What the hell have you *done* to yourself?"

Abby ran her fingers along one of her newly-plaited braids, long and thin and tight, twined through with narrow coloured streamers. She smiled. "Went into town yesterday and got them done. Cost me a ton to get my whole head like this. I've wanted to do it for ages; I just never got round to it."

"You look like . . . I don't know *what* you look like. You'll scare the guys off like that; you look like a crusty or a clubber girl or something."

"I *am* a clubber girl, remember?" Abby replied sarcastically. "Besides, the guys can screw themselves."

"Looks like they're gonna have to," Emma murmured resignedly. "None of them are gonna screw *you* after you've mutilated yourself like that."

"That is, like, *such* a massive deal to me," Abby replied, again happily sarcastic. "I care *this* much about what they think." She spread her arms wide, exaggerating the motion.

"Shut up about boys, anyway. I've had enough of them," Emma replied, and suddenly Abby understood why she was sitting out here alone. She sat down next to her.

"Rob dumped you, huh?"

"*No*," she replied, indignant. "We decided to split up. It was a mutual thing."

"No, it wasn't," Abby said. "He dumped you 'cause you used him to get back at Cal. *Back*fire, girl."

"Oh, cheers, I need your smug comments right now. What is *up* with you, anyway? You look like you drank too much tartrazine or something."

"No, actually it's because I've made a decision," she said. She looked at Emma. "I sorta think we shouldn't hang around with each other for a while."

"What? Why not?" Emma was aghast.

Abby looked sympathetic. "I've got this problem. I just don't like the people who hang around with you. It's just not me. Since I moved here, I've just been trying to fit in. But I've been kinda thinking, that's a bit of a stupid way to do things. Being something that . . . well, something I'm really not."

"You don't want to be friends with me any more?" Emma asked, her voice tinged with a mixture of menace and disbelief. It seemed to say: *don't you* dare *leave me, nobody* ever *leaves me, and if you do you'll regret it*.

"I didn't say that. I just don't want to hang with you. For a while," Abby shrugged. "You know, what you and me did to Cal was really crap. But I knew when to stop. I mean, I felt like such a *bitch*. But you . . . you really don't know when to throw it in. You've lost your bloody boyfriend over this petty revenge thing, and for what? Because he got you caught smoking? You've lost it. Lost perspective."

Emma was looking hard at her, unable to credit what she was hearing.

Abby stood up, looking out over the fields. "Look, thing is, I helped screw him up and I regret it. But you, you don't even care. I bet even now you're working out how to get him back even worse for Rob. I went along with you 'cause I was scared of going against you." She looked back at Emma and shrugged again. "Not any more, I guess. See ya."

"I don't believe it," Emma said, as she was walking off. She stopped and turned back.

"Believe what?"

"You bloody well pulled him, didn't you? The mumbling retard. You fancy him. You're going with *him* instead of me?"

Abby gazed levelly back.

Emma threw back her head and laughed. "Well, good luck to you. You don't half know how to pick the wrong side."

"Oh yeah?" Abby said nastily. She made a gesture with her hand. "I don't see any of your *side* hanging round with you this morning. Could it be that Rob and the other boys are avoiding you like poison, and so your little followers are, too? Seems I might have chosen the right side after all."

She walked away then, ignoring the insult that Emma threw after her. There, it was done. She took a deep breath, filling her lungs, and then smiled to herself. She felt a lot better now. It was time to be herself.

* * *

No, no, no, this was *not* happening, not to *her.*

Emma stalked through the corridors, empty for the moment but taut with the anticipation of the lunchtime bell. Her blonde ringlets bobbed behind her as she went, her anger obvious in her step and in the high colour of her cheeks. She was mad. Really, really mad. Abby. God, that *bitch.* It pissed her off just to think of her.

She wouldn't have been anything at this school if it wasn't for me.

Ungrateful cow. What, she thought she could just dump her best friend, change her hairstyle and then flounce away like a girl in a Bodyform ad? Sorry, but that wasn't the way it was gonna be. Retaliation was in order. Abby wasn't gonna get away with using her like that and then chucking her aside when she felt like it.

What got her most, though, was that her words had a ring of truth to them. As the day had worn on, she had found more and more that she was being frozen out. The boys had heard what she had done to Rob, and most of them – well, the ones who counted, anyway – didn't have a civil word to say to her right now. And the girls had followed suit, deserting her as unobtrusively as possible. The words that Cal had shouted at her in the corridor on Wednesday came back to her, circling her like vultures. *Why do you think all your friends hang around with you, Emma? It's not your charming personality. It's because you know all the* boys, *Emma.*

Two-faced slags, the lot of them. Screw them. It

would only be a matter of time before the boys began to forget about their little campaign of silence; after all, boys don't club together as closely as girls do, and even if Rob never talks to her again, the others will. Spurred on by their libidos, they'd crumble eventually. She knew how to handle boys. And with the boys, would come the girls.

But at the moment, it was so *humiliating.* And she couldn't believe how much it had hurt her to lose Rob. More than he deserved, certainly. But someone was gonna pay for that hurt.

All morning, she had been thinking of ways to get back at Abby, but she'd always come up with the same answer: no dice. With her crowd turned against her (temporarily) there was nothing she could do. But to get at Cal . . . now that was a way of killing two birds with one stone. She could hurt Cal to hurt Abby. And that was where she was going now.

Emma emerged from the school and was walking around to the science steps when the lunchtime bell rang. She settled herself on the steps and waited. It was only a matter of time before Cal came back to occupy his usual spot.

She was right. Barely a minute had passed before he turned the corner. When he saw her, he paled, then blushed. She stood up. Cal's eyes darted to the floor. He scratched his reddening neck.

"You know why I'm here, don't you?"

Cal could feel a horrible sinking in his chest. He knew. To gloat. Because Abby had fooled him, and she'd been playing Emma's game all along.

"You poor, tragic sucker," she said with false sympathy. "Shouldn't have messed with me. You shouldn't have called me all those things."

"I don't believe you," he said, the words straining out. "Not until she tells me."

"She said she couldn't be bothered," Emma replied tersely. "She did tell me that you got it on, though. Said you were an alright kisser. Personally, I think that was, like, above and beyond the call of duty. I never asked her to actually get off with you."

Cal was silent, looking down at his feet.

"What, you didn't fall for the story she spun you about how she hated me, did you? That's the *old*est. Good cop, bad cop. Good girl, *baaad* girl. We knew you wouldn't fall for the same trick twice. So we used a different trick. I was the bitch and she was the wounded angel. Oh, I guess you didn't know she was in the drama club, did you?"

Cal still didn't speak. He did know that. Joel had told him.

"How you feeling now, huh? Wishing that you hadn't split me and Rob up? Wishing that you hadn't got me caught for smoking?" She paused for effect. "Wishing that Abby could be bothered to dump you herself instead of sending me? Or just wishing that you hadn't suckered yourself into thinking that me or Abby would *ever* fancy someone like you?"

For a moment, Cal didn't move. Then slowly, his face a wall of stone, he walked away, past Emma, past the car park, and out of the school.

* * *

Suckered himself. Yeah, that was more or less it.

Cal was sitting in his living room, staring at the TV, seeing nothing. He had been like that for hours, ever since he had returned home at lunchtime.

Idiot. He'd thought all along that Abby was stringing him, but when she'd told him all that stuff about Emma . . . he'd trusted her, believed her when she said she was an outsider too. Shit, she was a clever bitch, wasn't she? After Emma, he'd been guarded. He'd not let her near him. But she'd been persistent, and she'd got under his skin in the only way she could.

She had been so *convincing*.

Drama club. His mouth twitched bitterly. He hoped they knew what a catch they had. She was a female De Niro.

He wouldn't have believed Emma, though. He knew she hated him. He wouldn't have believed her, if it hadn't been for the things she knew . . . things she could only have known if Abby had told her. About how Abby had said she didn't like Emma, for instance. And *nobody* knew that they'd kissed that night, that and more. He hadn't even told Joel.

But Emma knew. He pictured Abby laughing with Emma as she recounted everything that had happened that night. And inside, he felt the fire blaze.

After Abby had left on Thursday morning, she had gone into town and he had skipped school to drink coffee and bathe in the joy of what he was feeling. For the first time in a long while, he had been happy. And his need to burn had been forgotten, or had receded until it had almost disappeared. He had fantasized about her as his lifeline, his way out; he could stop himself, if she was with him.

Stupid. Stupid, stupid. And now the need burned brighter in him than ever before. For a time, he had abandoned the plan that had come to him, in that moment when he had stood outside The Caretaker's office. But now it was back on track. Abby and Emma could go and play their cruel games to their hearts' content. After tonight, he wouldn't care.

There was a knock at the door.

For a moment, he debated answering it at all.

"Cal? It's me." Joel's voice came through the letterbox.

He heaved himself to his feet and sloped to the door to open it.

"Hey hey, kid," Joel said, ducking and jabbing in an exaggeratedly matey way as Cal opened the door. "Heard about you and Abby Cohen. Way to *go.*"

"Good timing, Joel," Cal said glumly. "You know, if you open your mouth a little wider you can probably get the other foot in too."

Joel's face fell. "Ah, no. Don't tell me she—" he began.

"It was all a trick. The whole thing. Start to bloody finish," Cal said tiredly. "Come in, anyway. Want some coffee?"

"Stop it with the coffee, doofus," Joel said, concerned. "You okay? I mean, really okay?"

"Not really. Not at the moment. I'll live. Anyway, how'd you hear about it?"

"Chloe Potter told me. I dunno where she got it from."

Cal wandered back into the lounge with a sigh. Joel closed the door and followed.

"Does everyone know?" Cal said as he slumped into his usual cross-legged position on the floor.

Joel debated whether to lie about that, and decided that he really couldn't.

"If Chloe knows, I reckon pretty much everyone else does."

"Then they won," Cal said flatly. "They really got me. Over the weekend, they'll have spread it around that they suckered me. I mean, you've got to give 'em credit. It's such a good set-up. First they hit everyone with this big news, like the geeky little mumbling guy gets the hot girl, and then they pull off the twist."

"Ah, man, this isn't fair," Joel said. "You didn't do anything to deserve this. Come Monday, I'm gonna find that pair of cows and sort them both out."

"Come Monday, it won't matter," Cal muttered.

"What?" said Joel, not quite catching him.

Cal shook his head. "Nothing. I don't suppose you saw Abby today, did you?" He smiled sadly. "I've still got this kinda dumb hope that she didn't mean it or something."

"You know how me and Abby get along," Joel said. "No, I didn't see her. And *forget* her. She's not worth it. Stop torturing yourself. Come to Poppy's with me."

Cal looked up at him. "Yeah, and I really feel in a party mood. Listen to what you're saying. I'm not going *anywhere* tonight."

"Ah, come on. Drown your sorrows, or something. It won't be like last week."

"Yeah? What if *they're* there?"

"They won't be."

"Look, I'm not coming, and that's final," Cal insisted. He had his plan to carry out tonight. He wished he had just pretended he wasn't here when Joel had knocked.

Then Joel's whole tone and expression changed, changed to something that Cal had never seen before in his friend. His brash confidence seemed to dwindle, and he seemed suddenly terribly small.

"You've got to come, Cal," he said. "Those guys, the guys who beat me up . . . I still don't have the money. I can't get it off my parents, without telling them what it's for. And I know you don't have it, right?" For a moment there was a flicker of hope in his eyes, but it died almost as fast as it had appeared. "No, I thought you didn't."

"You know I'd give it to you if I had it," Cal said quietly. "My mum and dad haven't given me much since I turned fifteen. It's their way of telling me go get a Saturday job."

Joel looked morose. "I've gotta go to Poppy's tonight. I've gotta have one last go at shifting that draw. If I don't get them the money by tonight, I'm screwed. I need you to come, Cal. You've got to."

Cal shook his head helplessly. The *plan, the plan.* "I can't, Joel. I want to come with you, but I—"

"Look, Cal," Joel interrupted, almost pleading. "I know I haven't been a good friend to you recently. Not as good as I should have been. But I'm in *trouble*! I need someone with me tonight, someone I can trust. Someone who can call the police if things go wrong, or call the ambulance if I'm hurt, or something. I need someone there with me, Cal. I'm scared. Like, really scared."

Cal had never seen Joel like this. It was frightening to see the contrast between his usual self and this . . . *hunted* creature in front of him. Behind Cal's eyes, the fire was still burning, but this was his *friend*. His only friend. And like he said, he might have been neglecting Cal recently, but even so. Cal owed him everything.

"Okay," he said. "Okay, I'll come with you."

The plan could wait until tomorrow.

Chapter Ten

Alcohol

Cal was absolutely melted by the time they got into Poppy's that night. Joel was not far behind. Both of them had been drinking like desperate men, as if it was their last night on Earth. And to numb the pain of the kicking he was due, Joel joked weakly.

Nevertheless, by the time they swayed into the pulsing cave of light and sound that was Poppy's, their respective problems had become temporarily small and insignificant. They were both surprising themselves by having fun. They were scraping rock bottom at the moment, and there was a kind of strange release in the realization that the only way was up.

They weaved through the sea of half-lit faces, rippling and bobbing past them on either side. Cal accidentally burned some girl's arm on the end of his cigarette as she brushed into him. She swore as she recoiled, her hand flying to the spot where she had touched the glowing tip; but Cal had already wandered away, following after Joel, not even noticing what he had done. When he next tried to take a drag, he was surprised to find that the tip had been knocked off. He lit up again, his eyes on the flame, navigating through the packed dancefloor with something akin to sonar. An ascending puff of smoke indicated his triumph.

"Hey, check it out!" Joel cried suddenly, pointing to a shadowy recess on the ground floor, just next to the stairs that they were heading for. A couple were just vacating one of the padded benches that surrounded an empty table in the alcove.

"I got dibs on that!" Cal cried to everyone near by, sprinting across the intervening distance and throwing himself recklessly across the table, skidding over it on his thigh Starsky and Hutch-style and landing in a heap on the bench a heartbeat ahead of the group of girls who were about to sit there. Far from being pissed off at having their seat stolen, they actually started applauding.

Joel nicked an ashtray from a nearby table and weaved his way through the girls to sit down next to him, beaming a winning smile at them as he passed. They wandered back to their previous spot, conceding defeat graciously.

"That was slick, my man," Joel said, as he sat down next to where Cal was lying across the bench.

"I think I ruptured something," Cal said faintly, his voice muffled where his cheek was pressed against the bench.

"You know, this table's lacking something important," Joel observed, ignoring him.

"Alcohol," Cal suggested.

"Yes," Joel said, raising one finger. "I'll handle that. You sort out rearranging your spine. Back in five." Now on a mission, he raced off towards the dance-floor.

Cal disentangled himself, rested his elbows on the table, and suddenly realized that he still had a lit fag in his hand, which had survived even through his dive across the table.

"Still make 'em like the old days," he muttered to himself, dragging the last of it and stubbing it out.

Joel returned with the drinks, finding Cal guarding their table like a mother jackal protecting her young, glaring at anyone who came near.

"I am sooo wasted," he confessed as he put down the pints on the table.

Cal gurgled something incoherent in response.

"Better get on with flogging this shite," he said, patting the fat lump of draw in his pocket.

"Not yet," Cal said. "Come on, it's still only eleven or so."

Joel shrugged. "Okay, whatever."

"I'm gonna pull tonight," Cal announced.

"Wha-at?" Joel cried in mock amazement. "Could it be you've actually got loose enough to try it on with someone?"

"I dunno. Maybe. I can feel it, though. It's kinda like those old Star Trek episodes . . . if I *reverse* the *polarity* of my Negative Pull Aura, then, like, they'll flock. Or something."

Joel burst out laughing. "What the hell has that got to do with Star Trek?"

"You know, how they're always reversing the polarity of stuff, and. . ." Cal saw he wasn't getting through. "Forget it."

"I will, cheers. Oh, hey, that's . . . hey, Jo!"

He stood up and waved to attract the attention of a slim, pretty girl who was wandering across the dance-floor near by. She saw Joel and came over. Green, slightly Oriental eyes gazed out of a heart-shaped face as she leaned her hands on the table.

"Alright, Joel? Haven't seen you for ages," she said.

"That's 'cause you've been spending so much time with your bloody boyfriend," Joel returned, grinning. "What is it now, six months?"

"Five or six," she said.

"When are the rest of us red-blooded males gonna get a look in?" he said, flirting.

She punched him gently on the shoulder. "Don't go there, kid. You couldn't take the heat."

He laughed. "Try me."

"One day, space cadet," she returned. She caught sight of someone across the room. "There's that man of mine now. Love the hair, by the way, Joel. See ya, guys. Be good." With that, she kissed them both on the forehead and slipped away.

Joel sank back into his seat. Cal sipped his drink. After a few moments, they both looked at each other and licked their lips, making a lascivious "*Mmmm*" noise.

"Now *she*. . ." Cal began, trailing off because he didn't need to finish the sentence.

"Is taken," Joel finished. "Go for someone else."

"I don't want anyone else," Cal said eventually. "I want Abby."

Joel was momentarily wrong-footed by Cal's sudden change of direction.

"Uh . . . I thought you said you were on the pull tonight."

"Well . . . kind of. If the opportunity arises. Shit, I dunno." Cal drank some more of his pint.

"She's not good for you, Cal," Joel said. "Now don't go getting down over her. You're better off without."

Cal looked at him mournfully.

"Listen," Joel said, putting down his drink and leaning over in that way that indicated what he was saying was important. "I'm telling you this for your own good. 'Cause I'm your friend. And . . . well, without wanting to sound too much like a made-for-TV movie, *I don't want to see you get hurt*." He shook himself. "Urgh. Did I *say* that?"

Cal smiled. "The sentiment is appreciated, even if I should shoot you for the dialogue."

"Look, I mean this. I'm gonna be totally honest here. Like, when you and me go out, it's a real laugh. 'Cause we've known each other for so long, and we're . . . like, we have the same sense of humour and stuff. With you, it's not like with the other guys I hang out with. But . . . let me put it like this, right? You know when a guy gets a girlfriend, sometimes he spends so much time with her that he neglects his mates. And when he gets dumped, he's screwed, right?"

Cal nodded, unsure quite whether this rambling was

actually going to reach a point, or if Joel was going to talk himself into a knot.

"The point is," Joel said, with supernatural intuition, "I've been a git. And I'm sorry. See, because of, like, your *problem*, with being shy and all, it was sort of just . . . well, easier for me to hang out with other people. You know, it takes less *effort* to go out on a night with them. And it was a real laugh . . . I mean, it still is. But this whole thing with this bastard lump of dud draw . . . it sorta made me realize that maybe I'd gone too far in with my new friends and forgotten about my old one a bit. I guess that was why you were mad at me when I told you about the drugs. . ."

"Close enough," Cal said.

"Look, what I'm saying is this. I'd forgotten how cool it was when we were together. So from now on, you and me are gonna do stuff more. And I'm gonna *make* you break this problem of yours, I'm gonna *make* you come out and have fun until you won't think twice about it. And then you're gonna meet my other friends, and it'll all be cool. It's a mission, Cal. You've been going through a lot of shit, and I haven't been there to help you. I kinda feel bad about that."

Cal looked at his friend with big, fawningly grateful puppy-dog eyes. It was a kind of jokey expression, but they both knew that he meant it. There was something in that gaze, something like love but different. Call it real friendship, male bonding, whatever the buzzword of the day was. Everything was cool between them. That was all they needed to know.

"All that," Joel said, getting to his feet. "But first,

I've got to rid myself of this bloody meteorite of use-less crap in my pocket. You hang tight, kid. I'm gonna go and make a sale."

"I'm gonna switch on my chick magnet," Cal said. "They'll keep the bench warm for you."

"You do that," he said, but Cal didn't miss the worry in his voice. He was scared. If he didn't sell tonight, he was in real trouble.

Cal reached out and grabbed Joel's wrist. "Want me to come?" He knew he was too drunk to be any use, but he had to make the offer.

"Nah. I'll do better on my own."

"Okay. Good luck."

"Yeah."

He left, shouldering his way through the crowd, forging a path towards some of the other seats. Cal watched him until he was out of sight. He *had* to sell it. He *had* to.

When he was gone, Cal sat alone at the table, watching the dancers writhe on the dancefloor and listening to the rhythmic pump of the music.

Joel wound his way towards the clusters of tables, his eyes scanning the seated nightclubbers. He felt suddenly cold. It was only as he had got up from the table, only when he'd actually started looking for prospects to sell to, that he was really struck by what kind of trouble he was in. He thought about going back, grabbing Cal and just leaving, but that wouldn't solve anything. They knew where he lived. They'd even found him at Cal's house. It would only delay the inevitable. And his best – his only – chance of getting the money he needed was here, tonight.

He spotted a couple of kids, clearly under-age (like himself), wearing outdated Nirvana and Pearl Jam tie-dye print tops. Prime candidates. He wandered over to them, glancing around for any signs of the bouncers.

"You want any draw, lads?" he said, doing his best to make his voice sound street-rough and aggressive.

"No, mate," one of them said instantly; but the other said: "Hang on." They conferred for a moment, then the first one turned back. "You doing a fiver a gram?"

"That's the rate."

"Okay, fiver's worth. Let's see it first."

Joel sat down at the table, drew out the lump and his Stanley knife. Swiftly, he unwrapped the clingfilm and sheared off a chunk that was a pretty generous gram.

"That do you?"

"Cool," the kid replied, handing over the fiver. Joel pocketed it with no small measure of relief, wrapped up the draw and stashed it again quick.

His encouraging start, though, soon proved to be a flash in the pan. He met with little or no luck on the other tables. One guy even told him that he knew about "him and his shit draw". After half an hour, he was only twenty quid up from where he started, and still way short of the total. The night was getting on.

That was when he saw Sully and his lads, and they saw him.

He felt his heart sink. It was pointless running. They came shouldering across the dancefloor towards him. He spotted Weldon there, too, Weldon his so-called mate. Why the hell had he ever forgotten about Cal for mates like that?

"Alright, Joel?" Sully said. His short blonde hair had been gelled and combed loosely back. His blue eyes set in his square-jawed face conveyed a cold menace. His earring danced and flashed, reflecting the insanity of the disco lights. "You got my money?"

"I got half," Joel said. And he had raped his bank account for most of that. "It was the best I could do, Sully. Honestly. I've been trying to sell, but it's just not working."

Sully was looking at him flintily, his face hard.

"Look, I can owe you the rest. Nobody's gonna know that I was late paying you back. I'll give it you as soon as I can."

Sully shifted his weight on to one leg, looking askance at Joel. "Now you know that ain't the point, don't you, Joel? In my game, there's gotta be respect. And you're asking me to let a loan slide? That ain't a good way to do *business*." With that last word, he grabbed Joel and twisted his arm up his back, so far that Joel thought his shoulder would break. He yelled in pain, but the others were on him, pinning his arms, holding him fast.

"We're gonna talk about this outside," Sully said in his ear, and then he was pushed through the nightclub towards the exit.

Cal had fixed his attention on one girl on the dance-floor. She was giving it some, grooving and swaying seductively; she knew how to dance, alright. Not a looker, but Cal found her mesmerizing nevertheless.

He almost didn't see the minor disturbance that was moving around the edges of the nightclub, until he heard the tinkling of glass as someone's pint got knocked over. He glanced up, and at that moment an avenue in the dancefloor parted, and he saw Joel struggling, being dragged and pushed along by a group of lads that he recognized instantly as the ones from his house.

They'd got him.

Cal sprang up, pushing roughly through the dancers towards the disturbance. He didn't care about the scowls he attracted, or that the group of girls behind him had finally taken possession of his seat, rewarded at last for their patience. He was intent only on his friend. What he planned to do, he didn't know. He wasn't thinking that far ahead. He wasn't thinking at all, in fact.

Ahead, the struggling knot of people encountered the bouncers on the inner door of the foyer. Surely they would break it up? he thought. He stared incredulously as the bouncers waved them through, after exchanging a few words with Sully.

Can't you see they're going to beat him senseless?

He had almost caught them by the time he reached the inner foyer door. Racing after them, shouting, he was practically on top of them when he was suddenly grabbed by his arm and pulled to a stop.

"Where do you think you're going, mate?" one of the bouncers said, an enormous, shaven-headed guy.

"Out," he said, struggling. Then the other one

grabbed hold of him, a short, wiry guy. Bouncers always had to have one small guy among their number, who was invariably a psychopath and far harder than the rest of them put together because he had something to prove. Cal knew enough not to antagonize him.

"You're not going anywhere," the big guy said.

"What, can't I leave the nightclub? You're gonna keep me here all night?" Cal said sarcastically, incredulous at what they were doing.

"Can't have you going out there and starting a scrap with them lot," the little guy said in a northern accent.

"They're gonna kick my mate's head in!" Cal protested.

"*I'm* gonna kick *your* head in if you don't shut up and get back in there," the big guy warned, and together the bouncers led him away from the door and shoved him back towards the centre of the club.

Cal couldn't believe it. His friend was going to get a kicking outside, and there was nothing he could do to help. For a moment, he just gaped, his mind searching for a solution.

The phone? Could he get to a phone, call the police, like Joel had originally asked him? No. The phone was out in the foyer for a start, and that meant getting past the bouncers; and besides, Joel was probably still carrying enough draw to get him in a lot of trouble. He needed an alternative.

He found one.

A moment later, he was walking away from the bouncers, keeping his steps slow until they had lost interest in him and turned away. He headed for the toilets, as if to go inside them, and then suddenly darted down the dark tunnel next to them. The FIRE EXIT sign glowed green in the blackness. He stepped over a couple who were doing something he'd rather not think about, put his hand on the bar and pushed.

The door popped open a little. He held his breath. Where was the alarm? Where was the howling klaxon that would evacuate the club, and flood the surrounding street with people, so that Sully and his gang wouldn't dare kick in Joel for fear of witnesses?

Sodding safety regs must have gone out the window a long time ago. Shit.

He pushed the door open and stepped out. The fire exit came out at the end of a long, dark alleyway that ran all down one side of Poppy's, scattered with trash and lit only by the faint yellow glow from the street. It was where Cal had seen Joel last Friday, when he had been selling draw down here. Now he was here again, further up. But this time he was surrounded by Sully and his lads, backed against a wall, and none of them were interested in his drugs. They were a cluster of dark shadows, their faces made ghoulish by the side-light from the mouth of the alleyway.

He heard the thumps as the fists flew. Somehow, Joel was managing to keep his feet, probably propped up by the wall, but they were laying into him with such viciousness that he seemed barely conscious. Cal saw Sully drive a punch right into his cheek, knocking his head back against the brick. Weldon was there, too, throwing stomach punches when the opportunity arose.

"See, *those* guys in there, *they* respect me," Sully was saying, in a pause between blows. "Because they know what I do to people who mess with me."

"Bullshit," Joel said through puffed lips, defiant. "You pay 'em to let you deal in their club. Some respect."

Sully whacked another blow in his face, this one catching his nose and spraying a gobbet of blood from one nostril.

"Can't keep your mouth shut, can you?"

"Screw you," Joel spat.

Cal couldn't believe it. One half of him was filled with pride at the courage of his friend; the other was filled with horror at his stupidity.

Come on, Cal, do something.

But what?

"Oh, that's it," Sully said, suddenly drawing back. "I am gonna teach you a lesson. I'm gonna mess your face up so bad."

Cal's blood ran cold. A hunting knife had appeared in Sully's hand.

And in that sudden moment of desperation, the answer came to him. The plan.

"Stop it!" he cried, running towards them. Even through the drunken haze, he could feel the terrible shyness creeping through him, squeezing his chest, tightening his throat, making his skin crawl. But he had to fight it, hold it down, long enough to do what had to be done. Just for today, for this one last day, he couldn't be weak. He had to be strong.

"It's gun-boy!" Weldon whooped, as they turned to

see who had shouted. "Didn't you promise to mess *him* up too, Sully?"

"You got your gun on you, gun-boy?" Sully asked, turning towards him. Weldon and the other lad held Joel fast.

"Stay off him, you prick!" Joel cried, but was silenced by another punch in the stomach by Weldon that left him gasping for air.

"No, I don't have my gun," Cal said levelly. Keep strong, keep *strong.*

"Then you're screwed, too," Sully said, sing-songing.

"Wait," Cal said. "I can get you your money. And I'll pay you another fifty per cent." He waited for that to sink in, trying to still his shuddering breath. "I pay you, you leave us alone. Both of us."

Sully stopped at that. The prospect of getting the money back was enticing enough. It would save him a lot of hassle later. But another fifty per cent, in return for their safety? He would have done it for half that. They weren't worth the effort.

"You got the money now?" Sully asked.

"Tomorrow. Saturday," he said, his nerve beginning to break. "Outside Bishop Grove."

Sully's face hardened. "Tomorrow. Uh-uh, no way. Tonight was the deadline."

Cal was sweating. He was concentrating on keeping his voice level. "I don't have that kind of money with me right now. It'll take me a day to get it."

Sully appeared to think about that. "You know the place, Weldon?" he asked over his shoulder.

"Course I do. I go there, don't I?" Weldon replied. "Saturdays it's deserted. No security cameras or nothing. Only the caretaker to worry about, and he'll be no bother. After dark, it's as safe as anywhere."

"I can get it by nine," Cal said, jumping desperately to the advantage.

"Nine, outside the main doors," Weldon said.

"And if you're messing me around, gun-boy," Sully said, pointing the tip of his knife between Cal's eyes, "you and your friend are not gonna live to see another weekend. I know where you live. Both of you."

Cal didn't reply. He forced himself to hold Sully's gaze, unwavering. It was a contest of wills.

Eventually, Sully turned away. He sheathed his knife and motioned to Weldon and the other guy who was holding Joel.

"Let him go."

Joel slid to the floor. Weldon kicked him as he went by. They walked out of the dark alleyway and back into the nightclub.

Cal crouched down on one knee beside his friend. His face was a mass of bruises, and he wheezed his breaths in and out. He himself was trembling, as he realized the enormity of what he had committed himself to.

"We're a bloody state, aren't we? The both of us."

Joel managed a weak smile. "Thanks, Cal," he croaked.

Cal patted his shoulder and went to hail a taxi for them both. Tomorrow was going to be a long day.

Chapter Eleven

Combustion

Darkness had come down fast. Joel glanced at the sky, which was dimming to a charcoal grey-black, and then back at his watch. 8:40. His face and body still ached from last night, and violent twinges stabbed through him occasionally as one or another of his bruised muscles protested at their misuse. He should be in bed. He should have called the police. He shouldn't be out here, meeting with the guys who had kicked seven shades out of him less than twenty-four hours ago. He didn't have their money. And if Cal didn't turn up with the goods, then he was basically putting himself on the block for even worse damage.

He could still remember the fear that had raced through him as Sully had pulled out that knife.

He came up the track towards the school. Dark trees swayed their half-clad branches overhead, looming above him, rustling softly. His feet stepped through the shuffle of dead leaves, grinding them into the hard mud. Coming in from this way – instead of off the main road – nobody was likely to see him. He didn't know whether that was a good or bad thing.

It was all about trust, really. He had no idea what Cal had in mind. He hadn't been able to contact him at all. He was blindly placing his faith in his friend, and praying that he had something pretty special up his sleeve. Where Cal was getting the money from, he had no idea. He was sure that, if he had had it before, he wouldn't have hesitated in giving it to Joel to cover his loan rather than let him get beaten up.

So, where was the money coming from?

Whatever. At least, with Cal, he knew he could rely on him. Knew it without a shadow of a doubt. And even though he felt bad about lumping all this on Cal, with all his other problems, it made him feel good to know that he had at least one friend whom he could trust with his life.

Which, as it would probably turn out, was just what he was doing.

He crossed over the lower playing fields and crested the steep shoulder of grass that brought the school into view. It looked squat and ugly in the gathering dark, sprawling away left and right. He'd been up here before at night, getting pissed with his mates; it had been a sort of dare, to hang around the school and get sloshed. Then it had seemed harmless. But now. . .

Oh, for . . . just stop being a wuss.

He couldn't stop thinking it, though. Intuition or imagination, there was something different about the school this time. It seemed darker, more menacing. Like some kind of huge, lurking thing, breathing slow, massive breaths, waiting for him to step inside.

Joel shook himself. It wasn't even as if he was going inside that place anyway. They were just meeting outside. *Get this meeting over with, let Cal do what he's gonna do, and you can make a new start.* He felt the lump of draw still in his pocket. He could forget about ever selling *that* crap again. Well, no great loss. It had only brought him grief anyway.

He took the way past the bike sheds, coming up around the front of the school near The Caretaker's house. The lights were out. At this early hour, it probably meant that the house was empty. He wondered what him and his wife were doing. After a few moments, he decided that he didn't want to know.

Cal was standing by the main entrance, a pair of glass swing-doors that led into the reception. He was smoking a fag, looking out over the drive and the upper playing fields around the front of school. He didn't notice Joel coming until he was quite close.

"How you feeling?" Cal said.

"Like I've had the shit kicked out of me," Joel replied. "You?"

"Good," Cal said. "Better than I've been for a long time."

"You okay?" Joel said. Cal's response had been kind of strange; there was a steely calm in his voice that he hadn't ever heard before.

"I just said I was. Wanna fag?"

"Sure," Joel said.

Cal handed him one, adding: "Even though you've got a fresh twenty in your pocket."

"That's in my *inside* coat pocket. How the hell did you know that?"

"Seventh sense," he said, shrugging. "Sixth sense is danger. Seventh is nicotine. Told you not to buy twenties around me."

"You know, you should put those psychic abilities to use for the good of mankind," Joel said, hunching over the light that Cal offered, his fag wiggling between his lips.

"They'd only use my gift for evil," Cal replied, deadpan. "I prefer to stay vigilante; the terror of tight smokers everywhere."

Their banter was automatic, a reflex action; but today, it didn't seem to have much humour in it.

Joel dragged to get the fag lit, then drew away and blew out a jet of faint smoke.

"I was trying to call you all day. I even came round a couple of times. Where've you been?"

"Mum and Dad stayed in London this weekend. Most of the day I was out. The rest of the day I wasn't answering."

"What were you doing?"

"Preparing."

Joel paused. "Listen Cal, where are you getting this money from?" he said eventually.

"I'm not. I don't have it," Cal replied casually.

Joel felt a pit open in his stomach. "Then what the hell are you gonna do?" he said weakly.

Cal didn't reply. Instead, he flicked out his fag.

"Cal?" Joel prompted.

Cal turned around and pushed the glass doors. They swung open silently.

"I got it covered," he said.

"Cal? Cal, where did you get the keys for – oh shit, the burglar alarm, Cal! What about the—"

"Calm *down*. I deactivated it," he said, pulling a slip of paper from his pocket. He gave it to Joel. "The alarm code. I got it from The Caretaker's office. Same place I got the keys. He won't miss them." He took the slip of paper back.

Joel was getting severely worried now. "Cal, what are you doing?"

"I'd put that fag out before I came in here, if I were you," Cal said.

"I've only had a couple of drags on it."

"Don't want the corridors to smell of smoke, though," Cal stated.

It was a minor thing but Joel conceded, flicking his fag. It wheeled away in a spinning arc of glowing ash and skittered along the driveway.

Cal was propping the doors open with a brick. It seemed he had already prepared. Bricks don't just lie around in school corridors, waiting to be found.

"I don't like this, alright? Tell me what's going on, Cal. None of this mysterious crap. You don't have the money? What *do* you have?"

"I've got a plan," Cal replied. "Come on."

With that, he began walking through the reception, deeper into the school. Joel, after a moment's hesitation, followed. His sense of trepidation had increased dramatically by now. What was it he had been telling himself earlier to allay his fears? That it wasn't as if they'd be going inside the school? Kind of ironic.

"Okay, so what's the plan?" Joel persisted, catching him up.

"Listen, it's better if you don't know," Cal said impatiently.

"What? What kind of bullshit is that?"

"*Look*," Cal said through gritted teeth. He stopped and faced his friend, and his face was hard. "*Trust* me, okay. When I say it's better you don't know, it's better you don't know. Can you have just a *little* faith, please?"

Joel looked at him, surprised and hurt by his reaction.

"Okay," he said quietly, after a moment.

"Good. Now come on. They'll be here any minute."

Joel followed Cal into the gloomy depths of the school. His bruises throbbed and jabbed at him.

He was afraid. And what was worse, it was Cal he was afraid of.

Sully and his lads arrived soon after. They came up the same way as Joel had come, along the track and through the lower playing fields.

Sully was annoyed that he had let that kid arrange to meet them here. He reckoned it was because he was so surprised by the kid's offer of a hundred and fifty per cent. He shouldn't have let the kid decide the spot. He should have been the one in control.

It was also annoying, because it was Saturday night, and he and his lads had to get into town later on. They had a lot of stuff to sell, and Saturday was the biggest earner in the week. Bishop Grove was way out from the town centre, which was a pain he didn't need. Still, Weldon had his car here; they could wrap this up and hit the clubs by quarter to, if that kid or Joel didn't give them any shit. His patience was dangerously thin with both of them.

He felt the hilt of his hunting knife at his belt, positioned at the small of his back, hidden under his jacket.

Dangerously thin, he repeated to himself.

Weldon led them around the side, up some narrow stairs and through some kind of bike shed. He barely glanced at the little bungalow that nestled on a small grass rise, overlooking the driveway.

"Caretaker's," he said, thumbing it. "He's out."

Sully didn't reply. The other guy – his name was Emery – trailed along after, not really caring what was going on, just wanting to get into town.

They hadn't yet reached the main doors when Weldon said: "They ain't there."

"They'd bloody well better be," Sully replied.

Arriving at the doors, they found them propped open – a dark, cool mouth inviting them into the belly of the school.

"Now what is *this* crap?" Emery said.

"What're these doors doing open?" Weldon said, to nobody in particular.

"They want us to go inside," suggested Emery.

"Uh-uh, I ain't doing that," Weldon said. When they both looked at him, he said: "Are you *blind*? It's a trap, is what it is."

"Don't be stupid," Sully snorted.

"Look, they get us inside, they call the cops, and we get busted for burglary. It's bloody obvious what they're trying to do. They're setting us up."

"What, those two? Piss off," Sully said. "They ain't got the guts, either of 'em."

"Tell you what, though," said Emery. "I'm thinking that we really could sack the place while we're here. It's bloody gift-wrapped for us."

"Listen, I'm telling you, it ain't safe," Weldon insisted.

"Are there any cameras inside or anything?" Sully said thoughtfully, catching on to Emery's idea.

Weldon sighed. "No."

"School's got a lot of windows to get out of," he continued. "And it looks like they've already taken care of the alarm for us. If anyone calls the pigs, we can be out of here in nothing flat. They can't surround the whole bloody building."

"This is so dumb. . ." Weldon said.

"Alright, let me put it like this," Sully snapped, his voice suddenly aggressive. "I've come all the way across town to get this money I'm owed, and I don't reckon I'm gonna turn round and forget about it just 'cause someone leaves a door open. The pigs can't get us for anything anyway. All we're doing is trespassing. We ain't breaking and entering; look, the lock's okay. And we don't have a key. If anyone asks, we saw the door open and went inside to look for intruders." He grinned nastily. "'Cause we know how much you love your school, Weldon."

Weldon looked generally unhappy with the whole thing. "What about the drugs we got?"

"You can stash 'em somewhere, if you want," Sully said, shrugging.

Emery coughed. "I ain't leaving two hundred quid's worth of speed *anywhere*."

"Nor am I," said Sully. They both looked at Weldon.

"Come on then," he said eventually. "Let's go in."

Sully slapped him on the shoulder. "You're just being paranoid," he said. "But if those two don't have a bloody fine reason for pulling this little stunt, I am gonna mess them up but *good*."

They went inside. Unbeknownst to them, a pair of copper-coloured eyes was watching them as they did so.

Abby had been phoning Cal all day after she found out what Emma had done. He hadn't been in, or he hadn't been picking up. She suspected it was the latter. Just to be sure, she even found out Joel's number from one of her friends and rung him. She got his mum. She asked her if Cal was there. His mum said no, then called for Joel. She hung up. She didn't want to have to speak to Joel, especially considering what he must think of her. At least she had remembered the 141 prefix to the number so Joel couldn't use callback and find out who it was that rang.

So if he wasn't with Joel, she figured it was pretty likely that he was at home. Likely enough, in fact, to endure the twenty-five minute journey by bus. She hoped he was answering his door today.

What an unbelievable bitch Emma was. She knew just how to play to someone's weaknesses. With Cal, she had picked his low self-confidence. Abby didn't know the particulars of what had been said, but she knew it would have taken precious little to persuade Cal that she had been tricking him all along. He had been half-expecting it anyway.

Emma was a problem that could wait, though. She had dug her own grave, alienated her friends, and she was in for a pretty crappy couple of months until they started returning. Cal was more immediate.

She liked him. Why couldn't he believe that? She liked his meek, unassuming attitude, his quiet wit and sarcasm. She was sick of brash, arrogant boys who knew what they wanted from a girl and wasted no time in trying to get it.

It wasn't as if he was unattractive, either. Granted, he was no Leonardo di Caprio, but he was far more good-looking than he gave himself credit for. And underneath that fragile surface, he had unfathomable depths that intrigued her.

But he just couldn't believe in himself.

When she had got off the bus, it had been getting on for half-eight. She had written him a letter on the bus. At least, if he really wasn't in (or wasn't talking to her), she could drop it through the letterbox. Let him know that she'd been round, that she was concerned, that what Emma had told him was a lie.

The school bus lay-by was the nearest stop that she knew to his house, so she got off there. But she had no sooner touched the pavement than she caught sight of him, climbing up the shallow embankment that led from a small garage lot to the front of the school.

For a moment, she was going to shout for him, but he was still a way off, so she jogged up the drive towards the school instead.

When she was halfway up, she saw him unlock the main doors of the school and walk inside.

She slowed and stopped. What was he doing? What was he doing with the key to the school? Was he burgling the place, or what?

Curiosity and fear for his safety warred within her for a time; but she needed to know what he was doing before interfering. Otherwise, he might blow up in her face, and that would have the opposite effect to what she intended. She settled herself down behind the white slatted boards of the school fence, hidden by the growing darkness, and watched.

Cal came out a few minutes later, closed the doors behind him again, then stood around, apparently waiting. Joel was not long in coming. They talked for a few minutes, then went inside.

Abby stayed where she was, but the time ticked by and nothing happened. Eventually, her patience exhausted, she stood up to go in; but at that moment, she heard voices and ducked away again. A group of lads turned up. She knew them: Sully, Weldon and Emery. Nasty. They, too, went inside after a minute's deliberation.

She watched the entrance to the school, unable to decide what to do, getting more and more worried by the second.

What was going on in there?

"Here," Cal said, and brought them to a stop.

They were standing at a T-junction, where the corridor that ran from the reception joined on to the main corridor that ran all around the school.

"What's that *smell*? This whole place stinks of it."

"Polish. The Caretaker polishes the floors Saturday morning," Cal said.

Joel had been smelling it ever since he stepped into the school, but it was stronger here than anywhere else. It reminded him of something . . . but he couldn't place it. His nose was too swelled and clogged with dried blood to allow him to distinguish scents very well.

"Now what?" he asked, glancing around nervously before fixing a wary eye on Cal. He didn't like the way he was acting.

"Now we wait. For them."

"We do *what*? What do we do *then*?"

Cal, looking at his boots as if there was a shiny spot there, began to speak. "I had an idea, okay? My plan." He looked up at Joel, and his face was cold. "I was gonna do it yesterday, but you sorta needed my help so I put it off till tonight."

"What plan?" Joel asked urgently.

Cal ignored him. "See, it was all getting on top of me. The girls, and you, and . . . and school, and not being able to *talk* to people when I wanted to, and my mum and dad never being there . . . and . . . it just got too much."

"Oh God, Cal, what have you done?" Joel asked, his eyes widening, fearing the answer. But Cal just kept on talking.

"And then, after what happened on Friday, I thought . . . hey, like, two birds with one stone and all that. Let's get Sully and the gang in on things. Solve your problems, and solve mine."

"Cal, what have you done?" Joel repeated.

"I found the answer," he said.

Footsteps sounded along the corridor.

"Here they come," Cal hissed. "Just stay with me, okay?"

Joel couldn't reply. He had a terrible sense that something awful was going to happen, but he couldn't tell what.

Cal lit up a cigarette. He offered one to Joel, but he turned it down. Unusually for him, he was too wired even to smoke.

"I thought you said you didn't want the place smelling of smoke," Joel said, through puffy lips.

Cal shrugged. "It wasn't the smoke I was worried about," he said. "Now come on. It's best if we're not seen."

"But how can we—"

"Come *on*," Cal insisted, pulling him into a tiny side-corridor that led to the male staff toilets. They waited there, just out of sight. Joel's heart was thumping.

Then the pair of swing doors in the corridor opened.

"I swear, those two are *dead* when I find 'em," Sully said, his voice growing in volume as the doors swung out.

"They're not here. Look," Weldon said. "Let's go. We can find 'em later."

"I'm telling you, that *ain't* polish," Emery said from behind them.

"Then what *is* it, if it ain't polish?" Weldon snapped, exasperated.

Emery's eyes trailed across the darkened T-junction of the corridors. In the faint moon-glow from the skylight, he saw something he hadn't seen before. A slight sparkle, a glint. Something liquid. He looked down, and saw that a wet trail ran along the corridor past them, along the corner where the wall met the floor.

"Oh *shit*!" he cried as realization dawned on him.

A burning cigarette arced into the corridor in front of them.

Where it struck the liquid, ripples of blue and yellow fire raced outward in trails, one shooting past them towards the main entrance, the others going each way down the corridor.

They looked at each other, sudden fear in their eyes.

The next second, an almighty explosion blew them forward off their feet.

Chapter Twelve

Conflagration

"What did you *do*?" Joel cried, his voice hoarse with fear.

"Shut up and run!" Cal replied, pulling him out from their hiding-place and sprinting away towards the art department corridor. Joel ran with him, following automatically. Behind him, he could hear Sully and the lads swearing in fright, their voices high and panicky as they picked themselves up from the floor.

Another explosion rocked the school, booming through the hollow corridors, this one more distant but much larger. Joel and Cal sprinted through another set of swing doors, leaving the others behind. Joel looked around frantically, caught in the tumult of noise and motion. A way out, a way out, he needed a. . .

Then he remembered. Through the art department, through the technology block, and out through the fire door. He turned aside from their path, heading left.

"*NO!*" Cal screamed, grabbing him by the wrist.

"Get *off* me!" Joel cried.

"Not that way!" Cal insisted.

"Screw you! I'm—" he began, but he was cut short by an enormous wall of noise that erupted from the depths of the technology block, blowing the doors off their hinges. He felt the wave of heat and combustion even from where he stood. As the dust and debris settled, he could see waving fingers of flame peeping through the smoke.

"Come *on*! I know the safe way out!" Cal said, pulling him into motion again.

Too shocked to argue, he followed. Cal went ahead, a small, wild-haired guide, running confidently through the corridors. Joel ran after, afraid of him because of what he had done but also afraid to lose him, that he might be the only way out of the school. Another eruption on the other side of the building rattled the windows in their panes.

This whole place is gonna come down around us!

Cal swung around a corner and recoiled suddenly with his arm thrown up in front of his face. The corridor was ablaze, fire crawling up one of the walls, the paint bubbling and fizzing, the timbers blackening. Cal brushed his hair back anxiously as Joel came to a halt next to him, seeing with horror the blaze that cut off their exit. Then suddenly he turned to Joel and said: "Alternative route."

With that, he darted through the door that led to the inner garden, a small square of land in the centre of the school that was used for biology classes. It was closed off on four sides by glass-walled corridors; there was no escape this way. The black pond reflected the flames that gleamed off the windows, lapping upwards. Cal dodged along the rows of planted saplings to the other side of the small square. Swiftly he looked around, picked up a rock from the edge of the pond and threw it through one of the window panels. They skidded over the carpet of broken, twinkling glass and into a new corridor, away from the blaze.

There was another explosion somewhere in the school, this time a really big one.

"Chemistry storeroom," said Cal flatly.

"Hey . . . *Hey!*" Joel shouted, grabbing him hard by his shoulder. Cal stopped, shirking him off.

"Ow! What?"

"Don't give me *what*? You bloody know *what!*" Joel cried.

"Look, come *on*, you've gotta get *out* of here!"

"Not until you tell me what you've done!"

Cal looked about in agitation, evidently not wanting to waste any more time here. "It's the stockpiles," he said hurriedly. "I piled up anything flammable and explosive I could get my hands on, petrol, kerosene, gas canisters, volatile chemicals. You can buy all that shit from camping stores and garages; the rest I nicked from the chemistry labs. Then I ran trails of petrol to each of the stockpiles and linked them all together at the junction where we waited for Sully and that lot. I covered the smell by smearing the reception in furniture polish. Alright? Can we go now?"

"What about *them*?" Joel asked, incredulous. "You gonna leave them to burn?"

"I'm going back for them!" Cal cried. "First I'm getting you out."

"You're going *back*?"

Cal took a sharp breath, then obviously decided that it was quicker to explain than to argue.

"I blew all the exits. Including the main doors. Only one way out; but I marked them a safe route, okay? I wanted to give 'em a scare! I'm going back in once you're out. I'll lead 'em out if they're too stupid to find their own way."

"A *scare*? A bloody *scare*?" Joel shouted. "You are *screwed*! You know that? You're *sick*!"

"Whatever, just *come on*!" Cal cried in answer, once more propelling him forward.

Joel stumbled into a run again. This wasn't happening; this couldn't be happening! Cal was burning down the whole damn *school*! He should have known, should have at least *suspected* that Cal would do something like that. He'd been worried about Cal's unhealthy obsession with fire; but then his own problems had intruded, and he'd been so caught up with trying to sort out Sully and Co. that he'd forgotten all about his concern for his friend. Idiot.

There was a sudden crunch next to him, deafeningly loud. He saw movement out of the corner of his eye, and threw himself forward as a section of partition wall bowed outwards and collapsed over the spot where he had been a moment ago, its thin plaster surface rolling with flame. Up the corridor, a hail of glass exploded outwards in a lethal rain as another stockpile went up.

188

But he wasn't fast enough. He yelled as a burst of agony blasted up the back of his leg, swamping his brain, threatening to smother him and make him black out. He gritted his teeth and fought it down. Looking back, he saw blood soaking the calf of his right leg, and his trousers had been torn to shreds there. A heavy chunk of wall had struck him as it blew outwards, but miraculously he hadn't been pinned by any of the falling rubble.

Then Cal was back with him. "You okay?"

Joel could still feel the wind from the collapsing wall, which had missed him by inches. He didn't answer. He was concentrating on not screaming from the pain in his leg.

"Let's get out of here!" Cal said, grabbing Joel's shoulder. Joel cried out in pain as Cal's hand clamped over his bruised muscles, and his wounded leg shot a fresh pulse of breathtaking agony through his nerves; but Cal didn't let the pressure off, instead herding him onwards. He threw his arm around Joel, and carried him limping down the corridor.

The corridors were beginning to get smoky now, a fine blanket of poisonous fog that boiled along the ceilings. Joel didn't know the extent of the blaze, or how much of the school Cal had set fire to, but he felt fear surge into his heart at the thought of suffocating from fumes. Cal seemed unconcerned however, still possessed of that icy calm that he had exhibited ever since Joel had met him outside. It was unnatural. It wasn't *him.*

But who is he, really, Joel? He's just torched a school! Is he as sane as you thought he was?

They stumbled towards the back of the stage that occupied one side of the school hall, then turned aside through the PE changing rooms. Pelting through at a dangerous pace, hampered by Joel's leg, they finally came up against a red metal door that was usually used to let footballers out on to the playing pitch. Now Cal unbolted it and pushed it open. Joel almost fell past him and out into the air, grateful for safety, swamped with relief that he was not going to die trapped in a burning building.

"Get away from here, Joel," Cal said.

He turned around. Cal was standing in the doorway. His eyes seemed flat and dead.

"Don't go back in!" Joel said suddenly, because even through all this, Cal was still his friend, and he couldn't bear the thought of what might happen to him in there.

Cal looked back at him, his face so blank it was almost dreamlike.

"I have to," he said. "Bye, Joel. You were always my best friend."

And then he pulled the door to, and Joel heard the sliding of the bolt.

Were? What did he mean, were?

And suddenly a terrible thought struck him, crushing and freezing him like an avalanche.

"*No!*" he screamed, clambering up on his one good leg and pounding on the door. "*Cal, you bastard! No!*"

Ben Deerborn felt old and tired. The last week had worn him down. He'd thought that being back at work would help him get over the accident; instead it had just made him feel more weary and depressed. Nevertheless, anything was preferable to sitting at home and doing nothing; so he had doggedly signed himself on for weekend duty and overtime as well.

As he turned his dark green Peugeot from Grenfell Lane on to the main road, he reflected on what a mistake that was turning out to be.

Since Wednesday night, he had been thinking more and more about the kid. Cal Sampson. The boy had been growing on his mind. And no matter how much he tried to tell himself that Cal wasn't his dead son, the two had become almost inseparable in his eyes.

It was just a mourning reflex, he explained to himself logically. He wanted Carl to be alive still, wanted it so badly that he was seeing him in another kid. He was racked with guilt, and this was his mind's way of making things better. After all, it was *him* that had killed his wife and child, not the tree they had hit. Him.

None of it did any good. He couldn't help himself.

And now he was going to Cal's house to arrest him.

It had been on Friday that he had made the decision. Disgusted with himself for not acting against this (potential arsonist) kid when he had the chance, he had resolved to do something about it. In a way, he was trying to break the link between Cal and Carl; once he faced and overcame this stupid obsession, he could get on with his life.

It hadn't taken much. He had got a picture from his school files, and showed it to both Mr Watkins and Pan Adams, the farmer and the vagrant. Watkins thought it was him, but he couldn't be sure; Adams took some finding, but he positively ID'd the kid as being the one who was there at the factory fire.

After that, he'd gone around the camping shops, showing his photo to the staff there. The paraffin could have been bought at any garage, but there were only so many places where you could buy gas canisters of the size which had been used in the factory.

In Black's Outdoor Suppliers, he struck gold. Nobody recognized the kid, but they had recently had a delivery van turn up with an order for a large number of gas canisters. He went to the delivery company, and asked to see details. It had been paid for on a credit card, name of J Sampson. Cal's father, no doubt, and the card "borrowed". The delivery address was Cal's house.

That was all he needed.

But even as he drove to Cal's house to arrest him, he felt bad about himself. He felt that he was making a mistake. The kid was so frail and shy, just like his son. He wouldn't survive in a young offender's institution. If there was anyone he'd peg to be found swinging from his neck in his dorm, it was Cal. He would be a walking target, picked on by everyone until he snapped.

Was he doing what was right? Or was he just following the letter of the law because it was easier than making the decision for himself?

His mobile rang, bleeping in its charger cradle. He pressed the button to take the call.

"Deerborn," he said, changing down gear as he turned another corner. A small microphone near his head allowed him to talk hands-free.

"This is WPC Regis," came a voice. "Just thought you'd like to know. The fire department just received a call from a payphone outside Bishop Grove school. Explosions have been reported there."

"Bishop Grove?" he repeated, his heart sinking. "I'm on it. Thanks, Jean."

"No problem. Out."

He hung up and floored the accelerator. The car surged forward in response. Bishop Grove was not far from where he was.

He just hoped he wasn't already too late.

Abby found Joel slumped against the red metal door of the PE changing rooms. She had ran almost a full circle of the school, finding every entrance or exit a ruined mass of blazing rubble. She had no idea what she was doing, or what she hoped to achieve; but after she had called the fire brigade from the nearby payphone, she couldn't just stand by and watch the place burn. Not knowing who was inside it.

Exhausted, she swept around the corner and saw Joel. They had never wasted any love on each other, but all that was forgotten at the moment.

"Joel!" she cried.

He looked up as she ran towards him. At first, he didn't recognize her with her new hairstyle; but then her face slotted into place. "Abby," he gasped, hoarse from shouting.

"You look like shit," she said as she reached him. It was the first thing she could think to say; she was shocked at the bruises all over him. But then she looked at his eyes, and she saw them red with tears. "What?" she asked, suddenly dreading the answer.

"Cal's inside," he said. "I think he's gonna do something stupid, Abby. But I can't get in."

And suddenly Abby remembered something with crystal clarity, something that Cal had said to her on Wednesday night: *In a few days, none of you are gonna be able to hurt me any more.*

"Oh God," she breathed. "I think you're right."

"What are we gonna do?" Joel said. His voice was desperate. He was scared.

Abby looked around. "Isn't there any other—"

"Cal's blown all the exits. This is the only way in or out."

"No, look up there." Abby pointed to where a set of windows were positioned, high up on the wall next to them, to let light into the boys' changing rooms. They were semi-transparent rippled glass, set in flat rectangular frames.

"I already saw them. They're too small," Joel said.

"They're too small for *you*," Abby said. "I gotta try, anyway." She searched around, finding nothing suitable to break the window. Then an idea struck her. "Hold on," she said.

With that, she ran the short distance to where the skip full of gardener's refuse stood near the swimming pool, close to the steps where Cal sat every lunchtime. It had caught fire somehow, perhaps from the heat on the other side of the wall; but the blaze was still young. Shielding her face, she ran closer and pulled at a long, slim branch which was blunt at one end where it had been clipped. She tugged it out and stamped on the part of it that was burning, killing the flame. Then she ran back to where Joel was.

"Stand away," she said, ushering him back. "Watch out for glass." He limped a few steps away, and then she jabbed the stick through one of the windows. It smashed inwards. She ran the edge of the stick around the inside of the frame to clear away any glass that was there.

"Can you give me a boost?"

Joel hobbled over to her and knitted his hands together in a stirrup. She stepped into it and hopped up to grab the window frame, wincing as a grain of glass bit into her finger. Reaching through, she opened one of the windows next to it, swinging it open to its full extension. Then she pulled herself through that one. It was painful, and she almost got stuck when it came to getting her hips through; but somehow she made it, sliding on to the wide inner window-sill of the boys' changing rooms. Avoiding the glass, she slipped her legs through and dropped to the floor, before racing around to the red metal door and unbolting it, throwing it open.

"Nice one," Joel said, trying to come inside, but a stab of agony from his leg reminded him that he was wounded.

"Listen, you go out front and direct anyone who comes," Abby said, sucking her bleeding finger. "The fire brigade are coming. Tell them to come round this way."

"But I—"

"*I'll* get Cal. You can't help," she insisted.

Joel looked at her for a moment.

"Okay," he said, defeated.

"I'll be back with him," she said, and then turned and ran into the smoke-filled building.

Joel turned away, hobbling around to the front of the school. His leg stabbed at him with every slight movement. The patch of red had soaked into his lower trouser leg.

Out front, he slumped down on the grass of the upper playing fields and pulled off one of his layers of long-sleeved T-shirts. His whole body was a mass of aches and pains, both from the beating he had sustained last night and the injuries he had taken inside the school. He rolled up his trouser leg and inspected the wound; it was a gusher, alright, but it wasn't very deep, and it was already beginning to clot. Still, better to be safe than sorry.

Gritting his teeth, he pulled the arm off the shirt and was surprised at how easily it came apart. He tied it around his leg below the knee and pulled it tight, making a tourniquet to slow the blood. The bolt of agony brought fresh tears to his eyes, but he held them down.

The school was burning. From outside, he could see the extent of the fires Cal had set. They were beginning to break out on the roof of the school now, as the tarred surface heated up and ignited. Flames belched out of the windows of some of the blocks, spidercracking and melting the glass, devouring the wooden frames.

Once more, Joel thought: *Cal, what have you done?*

"Hey, you!" a voice called from behind him.

He jerked around, craning his neck from where he was sprawled.

Ben Deerborn ran up to him, squatting down next to him.

"Are you okay, kid?"

"Don't worry about me," Joel said. "There's people inside."

"Who's inside?" Deerborn asked urgently.

"Cal, Abby . . . three other guys. Go round that way and through the red door."

Deerborn looked over where he was pointing.

"Okay, kid. Ambulances are on the way. The fire brigade'll be here any second. Hang in there."

"Get *going*!" Joel cried.

Deerborn patted his shoulder once and then ran towards the school, thinking: *This isn't your job. Leave it to the fire brigade. You'll get yourself killed!* But he couldn't listen to that voice. All he could think about was Cal. Or Carl. Because, really, to him, they were practically the same person by now.

Chapter Thirteen

Incineration

Abby ran out of the changing rooms. The smoke was thicker now, making her eyes sting and her lungs hurt. The fire was everywhere. The air had become hotter, and she could see heat-haze mirages at the end of the corridor she was in, rippling like water.

Abby, what the hell are you doing here? she asked herself.

But there was no answer for her. Instead, she began to run. Cal would have to be here somewhere. She just had to find him.

The corridor beyond, a widening junction where several ways met and a stairway ran up to the maths rooms, was beginning to catch and smoulder. It wouldn't be long before it went up. She didn't have much time; if she went through, she might find her way back cut off.

She was so afraid. *So* afraid. But she was going to do it anyway.

She ran, not knowing what direction to take, just

going. The heat was suffocating. She passed the music rooms, which were as yet unscathed, and into a corridor where one side was heat-blackened glass, looking out on to the school's little garden. One of the windows had been smashed out, and a lumpy slope of burning rubble from a collapsed wall sprawled across the corridor.

No good. She turned back, trying another corridor. The banister of the stairs was beginning to steam at the top end as she ran back through the junction, her braids whipping wildly about her. She took the route that led towards the main entrance. She could see the flickering glow of fire in the reception area, but it hadn't yet advanced enough to cut off her route.

It might, though. It might.

She hesitated. She couldn't let her way back get blocked. She couldn't let herself be trapped.

It was that moment of indecision that saved her life.

A vast groan from above gave a mere second of warning before the ceiling collapsed in front of her, caving into the T-junction, vomiting a fountain of burning debris. She screamed, jumping backwards in shock, her hands clamped over her ears to block the awful noise.

You could have been there. If you hadn't stopped you could be under all that right now.

That was it. That was enough for her. She couldn't go any further. There was another way round, through the dining halls; but she didn't dare. The place was collapsing around her.

Tears beginning to gather at her eyes, as much from

disappointment in herself as from the smoke, she turned and fled the other way, back towards the changing rooms. But then she stopped. The assembly hall; she hadn't checked that yet.

The doors were right next to her. She darted over and pushed them open.

There.

Cal was sitting cross-legged in the centre of the empty hall. She had never seen the place so empty. He was just sitting there, watching the fire racing and rippling up the heavy stage curtains, with an expression on his face of such innocent, childlike wonder that for a moment, he looked almost angelic.

"Cal!" Abby called, running over to him. The ceiling was a turbulent swirl of thick dark smoke, and the fumes were getting unbearably hot. She seemed to be fighting her way through the very air to get to him, her hand shielding her face from the heat of the burning curtains.

"Cal, what are you *doing*?" she cried, crouching next to him.

He didn't answer. She shook him, but there was still no response. Then, picking up his right hand, she bit it hard.

"Ayah! *Shit!* Ow!" he cried, jerking away. That woke him up. He looked at her, bewildered. "What're you trying to do? Eat me alive?"

"What are *you* trying to do? Get a *tan*? This place is burning down, Cal. We've got to get out of here!"

Cal looked at her strangely. "I don't want to," he said.

"Don't be a moron, come on!" she persisted, pulling

his arm. He shook her off. She tried again. He stayed where he was, immovable.

"What are you trying to prove here, Cal?" she cried, exasperated.

"I'm not trying to prove *anything*," he said. "I'm just watching the fire. It's so damn beautiful. You wanna join me?"

Abby began to cry, tears of frustration falling from her lashes and down her nose. "Cal, you bastard, I can't just sit here and let you *kill yourself*!"

"Oh yeah?" he cried, suddenly shouting and getting to his feet. "And what's for me out there, huh? I . . . I'm a social outcast. I can't talk to people! I live my life just . . . with my head down, trying not to be noticed, living in fear of the next time I'm gonna freeze up and humiliate myself. I'm *weak*! It's pathetic! And I hate it! I hate myself! I don't wanna *be* me any more!"

"But *I* want you to be you!" Abby cried, then degenerated into a coughing fit as the smoke in the room seemed to clog her lungs.

He didn't seem to notice her discomfort. "You? Why? You're one of the reasons I'm in this bloody mess!"

"I never did *anything* to you!" she insisted. "Emma was lying! Can't you see that?"

"I don't believe you! You're still playing your stupid, petty games with me!" Cal shouted back.

Abby stared at him, then began to laugh, a bitter sound of disbelief. "You think I'd come in *here* and find you if I was playing a bloody *game*?"

Cal looked away, his face red with anger. He didn't have an answer to that one.

"Cal," she said, softly, pleadingly. "You can get over this. You can beat this. And I'll help you. But you can't give up like this. You *can't!*"

"Don't you get it?" Cal returned. "I can't *beat* this. I set fires, okay? I'm a pyro! You think that's *normal?*"

"You can get better!"

"I *can't* get better! This isn't just teen angst!" He looked away from her and said quietly: "I got a real problem."

"I know," she said, laying her hand on his shoulder. "I know you have. But there's ways of dealing with it. All you have to do is *ask for help.*"

Cal turned away, facing the flames. The heat from the curtains was scorching them as the fire gathered strength, but he seemed not to feel it. Abby's eyes were blurred with tears from the smoke.

"I never betrayed you, Cal!" she insisted. "And I need you as much as you . . . as much as you need *me!* And I want *you.* I like you and I want to *be* with you and will you please come with me so we can get the hell *out* of this place!"

And then Cal seemed to sag, and he suddenly looked frail, the icy calm gone. "I can't take being hurt any more," he said, his voice small.

"Yes you *can,*" she said. "You can! Because everyone gets hurt sometimes; the trick is in how we deal with it!"

Cal's eyes were straying back to the fire, to its mesmerizing yellow heart.

"No, Cal," she said, grabbing his jaw and turning his head back to her. "No! Look at me. Forget the fire. The fire can't help you."

She fixed his gaze and held it.

"If it weren't for you, I would never have had the strength to tell Emma where to go. And it felt *good*, Cal. But I did it because I thought I could rely on you to be strong, too. And you *are* strong; stronger than you think. You just need someone to tell you every once in a while."

She began to cough again. He didn't reply for a long time. The heat and smoke in the room were getting unbearable. The timber in the ceiling was cracking and burning. When she had recovered herself, she looked at him pleadingly.

"I love your hair," he said.

She smiled. Tears were tracking down both their cheeks.

"You came all the way in here for me?" he asked.

"Yeah, you idiot," she replied.

He kissed her, swiftly. They broke off, and he gazed deep into her copper eyes. Then he looked around the hall, as if seeing it for the first time. The fire was spreading alarmingly fast.

"I think we'd better get out of here," he said.

Abby's face broke into a great smile of relief.

"Come on!" she cried, leading him out.

"Wait," he said, beginning to cough himself. "There are . . . other people in here."

"Other people?" she cried.

"I left them a route out. I painted a line on the floor, a safe way through."

"What if one of the corridors has collapsed?" she said urgently, thinking of her own near miss.

Cal's face changed into an expression of horror. "Oh God, what if they *have*? I wasn't thinking! We've got to get to—"

"We can't! We gotta get out *now*!" Abby cried, and pulled him, and this time he didn't resist. Running through the heat and smoke and fumes, keeping low to avoid the worst of the vapours, they fled the hall.

Deerborn had shed his trenchcoat in the corridor. It was far too damn hot to take the blistering waves of rising heat that radiated from all sides. Vaguely, he remembered that he had his wallet and credit cards in the inside pockets. No time to care. Instead, he pushed onward through the unfamiliar corridors of Bishop Grove, a man possessed, heedless of personal danger.

Several times he found his way forward blocked; sometimes he found a way around, sometimes he had to backtrack and take a different route. He noted points of reference on the way, memorizing his way back with the characteristic attention to detail that had made him such a good investigator. He ran crouched low, knowing well that the heat and fumes were worst at the roof of the corridor.

Coughing and choking, he forged through the shattered, scorched arteries of the school towards its burning heart. Blindly searching, he knew that there was little chance of finding someone, if indeed anyone was alive in here. It didn't stop him. A fever had gripped him, driving him on. Where it came from, he didn't know. Perhaps he felt that his responsibility for his wife and son's death had left him owing the cosmic balance a couple of lives. Whatever the reason, he was throwing himself headlong into danger, searching for someone, *anyone.* For Cal. For Carl.

"Hey! Is anybody here?" he shouted

No response. Or if there was, he couldn't hear it over the cracking and warping of the school's death throes, and the greedy snarl of the fire.

It felt as if the skin on his face and hands was tightening like shrink-wrapping. The heat was battering him from all sides now, oppressive waves of unbearable, searing air. His shirt was plastered to his back with sweat, and dark patches had gathered at his collar and armpits. The world was a nightmarishly rippling heat haze.

This was hopeless. He would never –

Wait. What was that?

Voices. Or was he imagining them? Was it in his head, the fumes from the fire starving oxygen to his brain?

He had to find out. Breaking into a sprint, he pushed recklessly through a set of double doors ahead, coming out in a broad stairwell that led both up and down. He could see the glow of burning coming from below; not that way, then. Then his eye fell on the thick white line that ran along the floor, starting at the bottom of the stairs and leading upwards. It was painted in messy sploshes, and was still wet. Pausing, he listened, trying to concentrate through the suffocating atmosphere.

There! Faintly. Voices. Not crying out, but . . . arguing? Yeah, arguing frantically. From above.

He raced up the wide stairs. They opened out into a

short corridor, then doubled back and went further up. He kept on going, pushing through another set of swing doors. Bursting out into another corridor that ran away at right-angles, he heard the voices again, louder, nearer.

"I told you we couldn't get through this way!"

"Will you bloody shut up!" A voice, aggressive through fear.

"That kid set us up!" Another voice. "This trail don't go anywhere! The sodding wall's collapsed up here!"

"We're gonna burn in here!" The first one, high and hysterical.

"Go back the other way!"

"I thought you *knew* this school?"

"Screw you."

Footsteps, running. And then they rounded the corner ahead of Deerborn, stumbling to a halt as they saw him. For a moment, their faces were blank with incomprehension.

"Come on," Deerborn said. "I'll get you out of here."

Their expressions broke into naked relief, and he wasted no time in heading back the way he had come, pushing back through the double doors and down the stairs.

It wasn't Cal. It wasn't him. But he couldn't ignore these lads, now that he'd found them. He had to get them to safety. Then he'd go back in. It was the only thing he could do. He couldn't help himself.

Running back through the thickening fumes, he traced the route back to the changing rooms in his head, recalling it faultlessly. Sully and the others followed him unspeaking, unquestioning.

Deerborn jumped as the corridor ceiling suddenly split over their head with a loud rending, and his heart leaped into his throat. The timbers gave, and the tar roof above sagged in, but it held. He hurried his charges through, then ran past them and took the lead again. Behind them, the roof finally split, and a heap of melted tar and burning wood slid into the corridor.

Someone swore behind him. Ahead, the junction that they had to pass to get to the PE changing rooms was aflame. A display board was a sheet of fire on their right, the banister of the stairs had at last ignited, and the fire was licking up the walls, lapping at the roof.

"Stay here," he said. "I'm gonna see if there's a way through." Despite their bravado, the lads were too frightened to argue.

He forged on into the burning junction, shrinking away from the intense heat that singed him from all sides. He was almost blind from the tears that sprang to his smoke-irritated eyes, and he coughed constantly. There wasn't much time left. Not much –

And then the door from the hall was thrown open, and Cal came running in, accompanied by a girl with a cascade of thin black plaits. They saw him at the same moment he saw them. Both parties froze. Cal's hand slipped into Abby's. They were caught. Cal had been seen at the scene of the crime. There was no getting out of this one. He was going down for a long time.

But all Ben could see was their hands, clasped

together desperately, unified. All he could feel was relief that Cal was okay.

He looked at them for a long moment, with an incomprehensible expression on his face.

Then he turned away.

"Wait there!" he cried. "Give me a minute to check it's safe!"

Cal couldn't believe it. He couldn't understand what was happening. Was Deerborn letting him *go*? Was he actually letting him get away?

"Come *on*," Abby urged, unwilling to waste the opportunity. She pulled him onward, away from Deerborn's steady gaze, through the changing rooms and out, out of the choking school and into the fresh night air.

Joel was there. Cal fell into his arms, hugging him savagely, provoking a cry of pain from his friend. He pulled away, laughing.

"Sorry," he said.

"Haven't you got that leg seen to?" Abby asked.

"It's not as bad as it looks," Joel said, unable to stop himself grinning. "I had to make sure you got out okay." He hugged Cal again. "I am gonna *kill* you when I get better."

"Come on, we gotta get you to an ambulance," Cal said.

"Not from here," Abby butted in. "They'll ask questions, like why were you in there."

They both looked at her, bewildered.

"Don't you get it? That guy gave us a second chance. I don't know why, but he did. Let's get the hell out of here before you're seen. Joel, can you make it?"

"I got *pints* of this red shit left in me yet."

Cal began to laugh hysterically, and together, they ran, stumbled and hobbled away down the darkened track, and disappeared unseen into the night.

Chapter Fourteen

Ashes

Deerborn walked across the upper playing fields, coughing into his fist, feeling the blessed cold of the autumn wind on his skin, cooling the burning tingle in his forehead and cheeks. After getting some distance away, he sat down on the grass and watched the school burn. The darkness was full of the silent flashing lights of ambulances, police cars and fire engines. The fire department were handling the blaze, but it was more a matter of stopping it spreading than saving the school. Bishop Grove was gutted through by the flames. Nothing could save it now.

The lads that he had found in the building had been taken to hospital to be treated for smoke inhalation. They had been in there longer than he had; and besides, he refused to go yet. He wanted to stick around, bask in the newfound peace he had achieved, a calm that was only rivalled by the calm of the night sky above him.

The lads had seemed anxious to avoid the ambulances as well, even when it was clear they needed to be treated. In fact, they seemed to be trying to get away from the scene as fast as possible. Suspicious, Deerborn had ordered them searched, ignoring the protestations of the medics. The amount of drugs that he had found on each of them was enough to put them away for some time.

But it was the kid that filled his thoughts. The kid and the girl he was with. He couldn't stop seeing that handclasp between them in the moment that they were caught.

"Ben," came a voice from by his shoulder. He looked up and over, and saw Mike. The balding, portly officer sat down next to him.

"Mike," he said in acknowledgement.

"Heard about what you did. The sarge is calling you a hero. Nice one, mate," he said, slapping him gently on the back.

Deerborn smiled. "I doubt those lads are gonna thank me much," he said. "They were carrying."

Mike whistled. "What, guns?"

"No, drugs. Knives, too."

"Drugs? Much?"

"They were dealers," Deerborn said in reply.

"They set the fire?"

Deerborn hesitated before replying. "No. I don't reckon so. I'll find out when I do the investigation," he said. But he was pretty sure that the report would come back that he couldn't find a cause for the fire or the explosions, even though he knew damn well who had done it.

"You think it was the same firebug who torched that other stuff?"

Ben thought of Carl, of how frail and fragile he had been, and how like Cal he was. It was as if life had given him a second chance; a shot at redemption. He had known that Cal would never survive life in prison. He had also known that it was him who'd set those fires. Why? Because he was angry, frustrated at his inability to be socially normal? He would never know. But he had let that kid go, and he was going to drop the investigation against him.

Cal was what Carl might have been. The two, in his eyes, had become the same. He had ended Carl's life; but he had given Cal a new one, another chance. A clean slate.

And somehow, somewhere, he felt that a balance had been restored. An atonement had been made. He was at peace with himself for the first time that he could remember.

"Ben?" Mark prompted. "You think it was the same kid?"

Ben looked at the burning school, his eyes unfocused. All he could see was the way Cal's hand had slipped into that of the girl's. Togetherness. They had found each other. Unified.

"I don't think there will be any more fires," he said. "I really don't."

In the darkness, lit only by the funeral pyre of Bishop Grove school, the blue lights of the fire engines kept on flashing, a harsh and urgent rhythm that punctured the night.

And slowly, gradually, as dawn began to stroke the horizon, the fire dwindled and died.

About the author

Chris Wooding was born in Leicester in 1977. He's written several books for Scholastic, which keeps him in coffee, bad horror movies and Anime videos.

The author would like to say hi to anyone who thinks that the school Cal toasts in KEROSENE is eerily familiar. . .